Dear Reader,

Home, family, community and love. These are the values we cherish most in our lives—the ideals that ground us, comfort us, move us. They certainly provide the perfect inspiration around which to build a romance collection that will touch the heart.

And so we are thrilled to offer you the Harlequin Heartwarming series. Each of these special stories is a wholesome, heartfelt romance imbued with the traditional values so important to you. They are books you can share proudly with friends and family. And the authors featured in this collection are some of the most talented storytellers writing today, including favorites such as Roz Denny Fox, Amy Knupp and Mary Anne Wilson. We've selected these stories especially for you based on their overriding qualities of emotion and tenderness, and they center around your favorite themes—children, weddings, second chances, the reunion of families, the quest to find a true home and, of course, sweet romance.

So curl up in your favorite chair, relax and prepare for a heartwarming reading experience!

Sincerely,

The Editors

SHELLEY GALLOWAY

Shelley Galloway grew up in Houston, Texas, left for college in Colorado, then returned to Dallas for six years. After teaching lots and lots of sixth graders, she now lives with her husband and two barking wiener dogs in southern Ohio. She writes full-time. To date, Shelley has penned more than forty novels for various publishers, as Shelley Galloway for the Harlequin American Romance line, as Shelley Gray for Western historicals and as Shelley Shepard Gray for Avon Inspire.

Her novels have appeared on bestseller lists, and additionally, she won a Reviewers' Choice Award in 2006 and a Holt Medallion in 2009 and 2010. Please visit her online at www.Harlequin.com.

HARLEQUIN HEARTWARMING

Shelley Galloway

Starting Over at Lane's End

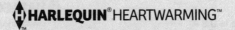

Recycling programs
for this product may
not exist in your area.

ISBN-13: 978-0-373-36618-7

STARTING OVER AT LANE'S END

Copyright © 2013 by Shelley Sabga

Originally published as A SMALL-TOWN GIRL
Copyright © 2007 by Shelley Sabga

Printed in U.S.A.

Starting Over at Lane's End

To Penny and Susan E.
To Kim and Carrie and Theresa, too.
Teacher friends who will know just what I mean
when I say that teaching school is a lot more fun with
good friends.

CHAPTER ONE

TWENTY SIGNS ON Campbell Road screamed the words *Lion Pride* in bold, black letters. A large black-and-gold cardboard lion, its tail bobbing in the bitter February wind, crouched precariously above the intersection. Three teenagers bundled in black-and-gold hooded sweatshirts darted down the sidewalk. Golden balloons bounced against a parking meter.

Basketball fever had claimed everyone and anyone in Lane's End, Ohio.

Everyone except for Gen Slate. She was trying to figure out how to navigate her Subaru Outback through the heavy traffic.

Drumming her fingers on her steering wheel, Gen wondered if she was ever going to get her errands done or ever get accustomed to life in her new hometown.

The past month had been interesting, to say the least. After resigning from her position at the Cincinnati Police Department, she'd signed on with Lane's End PD, rented an apartment and tried to get used to living and working in a small town.

Again.

It was a love/hate thing. Seeing people she knew at the grocery store brought back memories of growing up in Beckley, West Virginia. There, everyone had had something to say about her tomboyish nature... and how she'd never measure up to her big sister, Margaret. It had been a true testament to both their characters that they'd gotten along so well.

Gen thought of her mother, who'd never understood why she'd rather run track than dance in the pep squad. Why she preferred to go hunting the day after Thanksgiving instead of into Charleston for shopping.

Lane's End reminded Gen that lately she'd become fiercely independent, which was a real kind way of saying she was too standoffish.

Finally the light turned green. After turning down Cheyenne Boulevard, Gen counted another fifteen Lion Pride signs and spied two cars so thoroughly covered in white-shoe-polish peppiness it was a wonder the drivers could see at all.

As she edged her car along, she spotted a crowd of middle-aged men talking with a tall boy in a letter jacket. Team supporters slowed down their cars, honked and yelled out good wishes as they passed.

Gen wished the traffic would thin out. She really needed to get some dog food as soon as possible. If she didn't get an industrial-strength bag of Mighty Munchies home soon, Sadie was gonna go nuts.

After an eternity, Gen ran into Two By Two Pet Store and purchased Sadie's reason for living. She'd just hoisted the dog food out of her shopping cart to put it in her car when she heard a voice.

"Hey! You need a hand?"

Gen nearly dropped the fifty-pound bag on her foot. "Excuse me?" she asked, squinting against the bright sun as it descended in the west.

"Can I give you a hand?" the very masculine voice repeated. The man then stepped out of the glare and loped forward, *loped* being the operative word. His movements were so smooth and even Gen was sure the guy was a bicyclist or runner. "That's a pretty hefty bag for a woman your size."

The loper—or should she say *inter-loper*—had a lot of nerve. "I can get it." She'd never been one to lean on a man—or anyone, for that matter. It was far easier simply to depend on herself. That way she wouldn't be disappointed when things didn't go as planned.

But, as if he didn't hear her, the guy grabbed the sack out of her hands and tossed it into the back of her car. The action was impressive considering the guy didn't look all that brawny.

"You should have asked Ted to give you a hand. I'm surprised he didn't offer."

The store owner *had* offered, not that it was anyone's business.

The stranger's uncalled-for concern made her feel off-kilter and more than a little unnerved. Boys back home knew better than to open Genevieve's car door. The officers in Cincinnati had learned early on never to assume Gen couldn't do anything. The men she worked with in Lane's End were beginning to take the hint, too.

But this guy was treating her the way

folks treated Margaret—with gentlemanly concern. Because Gen had never felt very ladylike, the gesture took her by surprise.

"I'm okay," she answered. "Fine."

His brown eyes narrowed as he backed away from her. "Hey, sorry, I thought I was helping you out."

"No, I'm sorry. Thanks for the help," she amended, feeling her cheeks heat. Oh, her mama would be rolling her eyes if she were there to witness Gen's lack of manners. Even independent women should know when to say thank you.

"You're welcome." He paused. For a moment Gen thought he was going to say something else. Instead he shook his head and walked away.

Well, that prompted her to step forward. For some reason, she was uneasy about his assuming she had the grace of a bowling ball. Especially since her sergeant had just reminded her that morning about how police officers did more in Lane's End than uphold the law. *They interacted with the community.* And hadn't that been something she'd vowed to do better? "I appreciate your help. It's been a long day—the traffic is a killer."

"It is. There's so many banners and signs in this town it's hard to dodge them all."

She shook her head. "Basketball. I like it as much as the next person, but this craziness is pretty extreme."

The guy's lips curved just as she noticed that he, too, was wearing a black-and-gold sweatshirt. "You're not excited that Lane's End High might make it to the play-offs?"

Chuckling, she said, "I'm new in town. I guess I haven't caught on to the significance of it quite yet."

"You will," he said confidently. "This is the first time in twenty-eight years that Lane's End will probably go all the way."

"I'll try to keep that in mind."

Still grinning, he said, "Sorry—I have a hard time forgetting that everyone isn't fixated on the basketball team. At school it's all we've been talking about."

"School?"

"I teach algebra at LEHS."

A teacher. A math teacher. He didn't look like any math teacher she'd ever seen before. He was like Pierce Brosnan, Charlie Sheen and Clark Kent all rolled up into one. Gen had a sneaking suspicion that algebra was the most anticipated class at the local high school.

Because she was practically trapped under his dark-eyed gaze, she continued the conversation. "I bet you have a lot of interesting stories."

"Hundreds."

Gen knew this was the perfect time to tell him about her job. How she was the new police officer in town. How she hadn't meant to sound gruff or standoffish, she'd just never mastered the art of conversation.

How her mother had given up nurturing Gen's feminine side right around the time Gen had asked for a BB gun instead of a Barbie for her sixth birthday.

"So. You must have some dog," he said, pointing to the food he'd dumped in her hatchback.

Gen couldn't help but smile. "She is."

"What is she? Great Dane? Mastiff?"

"Beagle."

He laughed as he stepped forward again. "Some beagle. I've got one, too. Mine's named Sludge."

"Mine's Sadie." Forgetting all about not being good at chitchat, she said, "So I guess you know all about the trials of being a beagle owner?"

"Howling at night? Foraging for rabbits?" With a chuckle, he said, "I know it all."

As Genevieve thought about Sadie's penchant for snacks, pizza—anything off the dinner table—she had to agree. "Sadie once ate all the hidden eggs in a neighborhood Easter egg hunt."

"How many?"

"At least a dozen. She ate each one in a single bite. The colored shells didn't deter her the slightest." Recalling Sadie's bloated stomach and lingering aftereffects, Gen added, "I felt her pain for two days."

Holding out his hand, he said, "I guess if I know about Sadie's appetites, I'd better introduce myself. Cary Hudson."

"Genevieve Slate," she replied, shaking his hand.

"Genevieve. Pretty name."

Her mother had thought so, too. "Actually, I go by Gen. So is that Cary as in Cary Grant?"

"Definitely. My mom was a huge fan of old movie stars. My brother's name is Dean."

She was intrigued. "Like Dean Martin?"

"Absolutely." That infectious grin appeared again. "If you know of Dean Martin, you must be a movie fan, too."

"I am." Gen couldn't believe they had something else besides beagles in common. She had all of Cary Grant's movies on DVD and had watched the original *Ocean's Eleven* just last week.

She was warming to Cary Hudson, the teacher. Cary, like Cary Grant. He was likable and attractive. Open and approachable.

The complete opposite of herself.

At least on the outside.

Cary probably enjoyed walks in the park, hanging out in front of the fire, reading— activities that a lot of the men in her line of work didn't always admit doing. Sadie would love him.

Gen had the feeling she wouldn't be too opposed to him, either.

If she was going to be in the market for a relationship.

Breaking the silence, Cary slapped his

hands on his jeans. "Well, now that I've bored you, I'll see you around."

"I wasn't bored. Thanks again for the help."

"Anytime. Good luck with your beagle."

"You, too! And don't worry—Sadie's docile as long as she's well fed."

"Aren't we all?"

His comment was so true she burst out laughing. Cary joined in, then walked to his vehicle. Gen knew if she didn't say a word, she'd never have a reason to speak with him again—unless he needed help from the police for some reason.

To her surprise, hurrying home to Sadie no longer seemed that important, even if Sadie was probably entertaining a thousand ways to make Gen pay for coming home late for dinner. "Hey," she called out just as he was about to get into his car. "Do you drink coffee?"

"I do. Do you want to go sit down somewhere?"

Cary was obviously too much of a gentleman to make her ask him out. His manners made her regret skipping cotillion classes back in the eighth grade. "Yes. I mean, if you have time." Good grief, she was so bad at this!

"I have time. Do you know the Corner Café?"

"Sure. I'll meet you there."

Situated in an old yellow farmhouse, the café had already become one of Gen's favorite spots. She liked checking out the antiques there on Sunday mornings. It brought back memories of her mother's love of handmade crafts—and Gen's desire to be just like her until it had become apparent that unlike her sister, Gen didn't have a natural aptitude for anything handmade. After that, Gen had fostered her father's admiration by trying to be the son he never had. Unfortunately that hadn't really worked, either. Daddy had wanted a boy, not a girl who behaved like one.

That feeling of rejection still stung.

As Cary's shiny black SUV pulled out of the parking lot, Genevieve felt yet another jab of awareness. And of isolation.

She was lonely. She was sick of dodging late-night memories of Keaton, her former partner with the Cincinnati police. Keaton had been her first true friend in a long while. So true, she'd imagined he, too, had felt something special between the two of them. She'd been attracted to him from the moment they'd met, and had spent years waiting for him to notice her in a romantic way.

It had been incredibly embarrassing when he'd fallen in love with someone else, never giving her a second thought. The incident had been uncomfortable enough for her to want to start over someplace new.

It had been her good fortune—or misfortune—that Lane's End had been hiring. By the time she'd picked up and moved, Lane's End reminded her too much of Beckley for close comfort.

Funny how sometimes even a small town could seem too big.

CARY SHIFTED HIS Explorer into fourth gear and wondered what in the world he was doing meeting Gen for coffee. Even if she did look like a sporty Demi Moore, his instincts told him he had no business even thinking about another relationship after his ex, Kate Daniels, had taken his heart and pulverized it by the time she'd been through with him.

Still, Cary supposed he should thank Kate for opening his eyes. He'd no longer assume anything in a relationship. *I love you* sometimes only meant "I want to go to bed with you." *I want a relationship* didn't necessarily mean love was on a woman's mind. No, it might just mean "I want you… until someone better comes along."

He'd spent the past three months volunteering on too many committees at Lane's End High, helping his brother's daughter, Melissa, and trying to forget he'd ever fallen in love with Kate.

So what was he doing meeting Genevieve at a coffee shop?

Because there'd been something in her eyes that broke his heart. She looked as if she needed a friend. That, he could do.

After they both arrived at the café, Cary guided her to an empty table and flagged over the waitress. She quickly took their orders, then disappeared.

As Gen slipped their menus back in the holder at the end of the table, she looked pretty pleased with herself.

Cary was intrigued. "What's the joke?"

Her smile widened. "Oh, nothing, really. I'm just feeling pretty proud of myself for not ordering any of the pastries on the menu. Ordinarily, I'd have had an éclair or two."

"You've got a sweet tooth?"

"One about the size of Alaska."

He laughed. "It's been a while since I've been with a woman who wasn't constantly worried about every morsel she ingested."

"That sure isn't me! I tend to worry about other things." A shadow crossed her face. "Like this. I don't usually ask men I've just met to coffee."

"Then we're even. I don't usually get asked out at the pet store." When her eyes widened, he added hastily, "Good thing it's just coffee, huh?"

She relaxed visibly. "Yeah. Good thing."

Hoping to set her at ease, Cary asked, "So, what do you do for a living?"

"I'm a cop."

"Yeah?" Taking in her form, Cary had to admit the occupation fit. Tall and athletic, her personality strong and assertive, Gen Slate looked born to the job. "I've never known a cop before. I mean, beyond the occasional parking or speeding ticket. What kind of cop are you? Traffic? Vice? Homicide?"

"You've been watching too many detective shows," she said, her dark blue eyes brightening. "In a town like Lane's End we do everything that's needed. Luckily there isn't much need for a homicide unit."

After the server delivered their drinks, Gen sipped hers delicately. That purely feminine trait intrigued him. "So…" he prodded.

"I just joined the local police department. I was on patrol in Cincinnati for five years. Now I'm learning to adjust to small-town life. Again."

"How's it going?"

"So far, so good. I'm beginning to realize change is a good thing."

He'd heard that, too, which made him wonder why he'd been so complacent for so long. Maybe it was time to think about other things besides dating women he'd known for years, work and family obligations.

Maybe it was time to shake things up a bit.

"Most of my day is spent handling regular stuff," Gen said. "Domestic disputes. Kids drinking and driving. The occasional traffic stop." Pausing, she added, "I bet I've unlocked more car doors and investigated more dog-barking violations in the past month than I did during the whole time in CPD."

"I'm fascinated."

"You're nuts!" she exclaimed with a laugh. "Being a cop is *not* fascinating. But I do love the job. I'd go crazy if I had to sit at a desk all day."

"I feel the same way about my job. Teaching high school assures me that I'll never have a dull moment."

"I guess you can get pretty attached to your students."

Cary nodded as he thought of the fine line he walked between confidant and authority figure at Lane's End High. "I have gotten to know quite a few of them well. Some need another person who cares about their lives…others just need someone to listen. It comes with the territory."

Genevieve relaxed and realized with some surprise that she was enjoying herself. Cary was interesting and easy to talk to. Maybe this little coffee date would lead to another date. And another.

Maybe then she'd forget all about Keaton. Maybe—

The sharp ring of her cell phone broke through that little daydream. "Sorry, I've got to answer this," she murmured when she saw it was the precinct calling. "Slate."

"I know you're off the clock, but we need some backup on east I-275. You anywhere near there?" Allison, the dispatcher on duty, asked.

With a frown, Gen mentally figured how far she was from the highway. "Five minutes. Eight tops."

"Good." With practiced, measured tones, Allison launched into details about the accident.

Gen processed the information quickly. "I'm on my way."

"Problem?" Cary asked, standing up as she did.

"Yeah, sorry." Quickly she fished for a

five in her jeans pocket. "Here. I've got to—"

"Save your money. My treat." When she looked at him in surprise, he added, "It's just coffee, Slate. No big deal."

Though she knew he was right, Gen felt her spirits deflate. *Slate*. Men who wanted to be only friends called women by their last names. For a brief moment she'd hoped they could have been more.

As she strode to her car, Gen realized she was glad she'd taken the time to get to know Cary Hudson. Even if they never saw each other again, it had been good to put herself out there and meet new people.

Gen also had a feeling that Sadie was probably worming her way out of her metal kennel at that very moment, irritated her Mighty Munchies were nowhere in sight.

As Gen imagined a hungry Sadie foraging in the kitchen unsupervised, she hoped she'd remembered to shut the pantry door.

CHAPTER TWO

CARY WROTE THE last of the theorem on the whiteboard, then turned to face his class. "Don't forget to refer to these notes when you do page one hundred fifty-six for homework."

As expected, groans erupted across the room. There was a big pep rally planned for the afternoon as the basketball team was now two games away from making the district finals. Glancing at the clock, he feigned surprise. "Would you look at that? I must have miscalculated the time. We still have fifteen minutes of class. Some of you might be able to get the majority of the assignment done before the bell."

Almost simultaneously, twenty pencils hit the desks. Well, twenty pencils except for the one belonging to Amy Blythe, the curly-haired blonde in the front row. "I don't think you know how to miscalculate, Mr. Hudson."

Because he was no actor, Cary merely smiled and motioned to the clock over the whiteboard. "There's thirteen minutes left of class, Amy."

Taking the hint, she, too, buried her face in the math book. Cary used the time to erase the board for the following day, then take a quick tour of the room to make sure everyone was on the right page. He'd learned his first year that just because *he* was on task it didn't mean all his students were.

As he nodded, pointed to correct answers and high-fived the kids who finished, he thought again about something that was the complete opposite of math and equations— Genevieve Slate. The cop. Total brunette perfection. He'd been mesmerized the moment she'd tromped out of the pet store, full of determination.

She'd been all business and grit. Though not really. There'd been a flash of vulnerability in her blue eyes, as if someone had hurt her. He knew the feeling well.

Sitting on the edge of his desk, he waited for the last three minutes of class to tick by.

One of the boys near the front caught his eye. "Mr. Hudson, you going to the game?"

"Of course."

In the back row, Ben Schultz raised his head. "I heard Jamestown's pretty good. I hope we'll have a chance."

Cary hid a smile. Until recently, Ben had only paid attention to computers and science labs. It looked as if everyone—teachers, students and townsfolk—was rallying behind the Lions. "Brian McCullough's pretty good, too," he said, referring to their team's star forward.

"He's better than that, Mr. Hudson," Amy chimed in. "College scouts have been to the last four games. I heard he's about to get offered a scholarship to Ohio State."

"You know more than I do. I hope he gets it."

"Amy likes him," Jeremy called out snidely. "Too bad he's dating Melissa."

Cary wisely said nothing. Amy lived down his street, and Melissa was his niece.

"*Everyone* likes Brian McCullough,"

Amy retorted, though her cheeks flushed with embarrassment.

A couple more books closed just as the bell rang.

"Thanks, Mr. Hudson," a few kids called out as they ran out the door.

"No problem. See you tomorrow."

"See you *tonight,*" Jeremy corrected with a grin.

"That's right. I'll see you tonight."

One by one they filed out, leaving the room empty in seconds. Cary wandered back to his desk and sat down just as his best friend, Dave Fanning, strode in.

"Want to grab a burger before the game?"

"Sure, but I have to run home first and take care of Sludge."

Dave scowled. "How is that crazed dog?"

"Great."

"He tore up my new pair of loafers last time I was at your place."

"You've been warned. All shoes are fair game if they're not on someone's feet."

"Why didn't you get a Lab like most normal people? I've never heard of a Labrador having a wool-and-shoe fetish."

"No Labs at the pound."

"Just psycho beagles."

"He's only three-quarters beagle. The rest is a mystery."

"I'd bet money he's one-fourth rottweiler." After nodding to another teacher who walked by, Dave directed a look Cary's way. "So have you signed next year's contract yet?"

"Nope."

"It's due by next Friday."

"I'll make my decision by then."

Dave leaned against the doorjamb. A parade of noisy kids passed behind him. "Why are you waiting? Is it because of Kate? She's moved on, you know. What was between you two is history."

"This next contract is for three years. I just want to make sure this is where I want to be."

"You've lived here all your life. Where else would you want to be?"

Nowhere, but was he ready to decide that there was no other place he wanted to be than Lane's End? "I'll probably sign it. I'm just not in a hurry this year. And, Dave, I don't care that Kate is dating Michael Kent." The jerk.

"He deserves her," Dave scoffed, making no effort to hide his feelings for either of them. "But, for your information, Michael has just had his second interview in Lakota."

Lakota was a large and steadily growing district to the west.

That was news. "Really?"

"He wants a principalship. No way is he going to get one around here anytime soon."

Cary knew that to be true. Lane's End had just two elementary schools, one junior high and one high school. It was small town all the way. The only time administrators left their positions was when they died or retired, and Evan Miller, the principal of Lane's End, was years away from either. "When's he supposed to hear something?"

"Any day."

"Thanks for the update."

"So…food?"

"Yeah, sure. I'll meet you at the Cheyenne Shack in about an hour."

Dave grinned. "Good." He looked as

though he was about to say more when Melissa stuck her head in.

"Uncle Cary, you still going to the game tonight?"

"Yep. You cheering tonight?"

Melissa laughed. "Of course. See you there."

Cary raised a hand in goodbye as she flashed him a smile before disappearing.

"You've got to stay at LEHS," Dave said when they were alone again. "The whole student body loves you. You're the most popular teacher on campus."

"Pretty impressive for a math geek, huh?"

Since he and Dave had known each other since their own high school days and had even roomed together in college, his friend rolled his eyes. "Too impressive for you," he retorted. "See you at the Shack."

"GIVE ME AN *L!* GIVE me an *A!* Give me an *N!*" a peppy blonde with the loudest voice in the world screamed to the filled-to-capacity gymnasium. Obediently the crowd called out the letters in unison, most waving black-and-gold pom-poms.

"This is giving me a headache," Gen told Sam Clark as they passed the exuberant cheerleaders and made their way up the stands. "I can't believe you conned me into coming."

"*Conned* you? This is the biggest thing going tonight. Lane's End's basketball team hasn't done this well in years. If we win tonight and the next game, we're in the play-offs."

"I know. I'm excited for the kids, too. And the whole town. It's just a little over-whelming."

"For you?" Sam looked surprised. "And here I thought our newest member of the force was invincible."

Gen laughed at Sam's exaggeration. Sam was one of the few members of the force who hadn't closed ranks against the new female officer. Instead he'd done his best to be available for all of her questions. They'd hit it off so well, when he'd asked if she wanted a lift to the game, she'd said yes. Sam's girlfriend, Meagan, lived in Dayton, so he was a perfect date for Gen—a friend who wasn't interested in anything more.

Sliding down the bleacher, Gen said, "I

have to admit I would have been perfectly okay hearing all about it in the paper tomorrow."

"Not half as fun. Besides, think of this as your civic duty. Half the town is here," Sam said as they claimed one of the last empty spots. "It's a great time to meet new people and socialize. Before you know it, you'll feel like you're a part of the community."

Gen doubted it would be easy. She'd always felt a little apart from everyone, but the distance was almost comfortable. It was a lot easier to depend on herself than on other people.

As a cheerleader dressed in a furry Lions costume appeared and everyone went nuts, Gen figured Sam had been right. It did seem as if half the populace was crammed into the high school gym. As she scanned the crowd, Gen recognized a few of the faces. There was the chief of police. The mayor. Her new vet. Cary Hudson.

Her pulse sped up as she spied him smiling at a mom and two toddlers.

Surprised at her reaction, Gen tamped it down with effort. Of course Cary was there. Hadn't he admitted how excited he was about the play-offs? Besides, some of his students were probably on the team.

Narrowing her eyes, she had to admit he looked just as handsome from across a gym floor as he had sitting across a table from her. A sharp feeling of regret stabbed deep as Gen realized she should've asked for his number or passed on her email address.

Though by the looks of things, it didn't seem as if he needed another friend. No, the guy was swamped with attention, talking to five or six people at the same time. Two men about his age sat on one side of him; high school kids flanked his right side. Genevieve couldn't resist grinning. Dressed in a black long-sleeved T-shirt, he looked relaxed and happy.

She was just about to turn away when he glanced across the sea of people and caught her eye. When he raised a hand in greeting, she did the same.

"Who are you waving at?" Sam asked.

"The guy in the long-sleeved black shirt. Cary Hudson. He's a math teacher here."

"I know Cary," Sam said.

"How do you know him?"

Sam shrugged. "This is Lane's End, remember? My sister used to date his brother. Cary's a nice guy."

"He sure looks popular."

"He is, I guess. Cary's one of those people who just seems content, you know? Never seen him flustered." Sam nodded to a couple sitting two rows down before continuing. "His dad was a minister. Did you know that?"

"No. I just met him the other day."

"Well, Paul Hudson was a pastor for almost three decades before he passed away. Cary's brother, Dean, is a financial advisor. He and his daughter, Melissa, live right next door to Cary in their parents' old house."

"That's pretty unusual, two brothers living side by side."

Sam nodded. "From what I've been told, it works out well. Dean's wife took off when Melissa was just a baby, so Cary watched her during summer breaks."

Gen wished she had that kind of close relationship with Margaret. But more distanced them than miles. For most of her life, Gen had been career-oriented, doing her best to achieve recognition as a cop, while Meg was a wife and mother to three kids. It was what Meg had always wanted since getting her first doll. Those goals had seemed to divide them. Gen wondered if they could ever find common ground.

Gen peeked over at Cary again, but he was gone. Curious, she scanned the crowd, but it was hard to find anything in the sea of black and gold.

Then she spied him walking toward her up the narrow passage in between the rows of bleachers. As he approached, her stomach clenched. The feeling was awkwardly familiar—she'd felt the same way standing outside her captain's office.

Cary, on the other hand, looked as though he had no such qualms at all. He was working the crowd like a seasoned politician, greeting everyone by name, shaking hands, joking with a crowd of boys who'd sprayed their hair bright yellow for the game.

"Hey, Sam. Hey, Gen." Pointing to the Lane's End Lions sweatshirt Sam had given her, he said, "Looks like you've finally caught the fever, too."

"I've caught something," she murmured

just as Sam trotted down the bleachers to "socialize," leaving his spot to Cary.

"Mind if I join you?" he asked.

"Not at all." Eyeing some kids eating candy bars two rows down, she said, "I was just sitting here, wondering if I needed to get myself a Snickers bar."

He laughed as he sat down next to her. "I'd offer you one, but all I've got is a pack of Big Red."

"You offering?"

Pulling out a stick of gum, he placed it in her hand. "Of course. I'd never refuse a cop."

The light flirtation made Gen smile. That it centered around her penchant for junk food kept things nice and easy. "I knew you were as smart as you looked," she teased.

"I'm smarter," he countered, unwrapping a piece for himself.

As the crowd roared again, Gen popped the gum in her mouth and told herself that there was nothing brewing between her and Cary Hudson. Nothing more than friendship.

Yeah, right.

CHAPTER THREE

"Go, Lions!" the cheerleaders yelled in unison. "Go, Lane's End!"

The crowd roared to life as the team came on the court. Hoots and hollers abounded as everyone leaped to their feet. But though he'd been looking forward to the game, suddenly all Cary wanted to do was stare at Gen Slate. She looked cute in a sweatshirt and jeans, her long black hair tied in a ponytail.

"How's Sadie?"

"Rotten," she said with a grin. "The day I saw you, she escaped from her kennel, nudged open the pantry door and ate two boxes of cereal before I came home. What about Sludge?"

"He's the same as always. Last night he attacked the football I was throwing and howled at the mail carrier."

Recalling how harried Gen had looked

when she'd left the café, he said, "Was everything okay after your call? You left in a hurry."

"More or less. A semi had collided with a car on I-275 and the department needed some support." Eyes clouding, Gen shook her head. "It was touch and go for a while, but everyone involved ended up okay."

"Glad to hear it."

Gen gestured to Sam. "I heard you and Sam know each other."

"We do." Cary laughed. "I think everyone here pretty much knows each other. And their mothers, fathers and grade-school teachers."

"He said your father was with the church."

"Yeah. A minister." Interested in finding out why she was asking, he said, "Are you looking for a church or something?"

"Oh my goodness, no."

Her tone took him off guard. "Okay," he answered, drawing out the word.

"Sorry, I guess that came out wrong. I meant to say I've never had time for that kind of stuff."

Though her tone was light, Cary caught the edge of steel in it. "I see."

She glanced his way again, all big blue eyes and wariness. "Hey, I hope I didn't offend you."

"Not at all." He wasn't offended…just disappointed. Gen Slate seemed covered in a hard shell, giving him little idea about what she was really like.

Did he really want to become involved with another woman who wasn't honest about her feelings?

As he spied Dave and saw that his brother was now sitting with him, Cary stood. "Well, it was good to see you. I'm going to head on back and let Sam reclaim his seat."

"Oh. All right."

Cary's heart softened as he noticed that same touch of confusion in her eyes he'd spied at the pet store. "Hey, be careful on patrol, Gen."

A flash of humor—and vulnerability?—crossed her face before she tamped it down. "Don't worry, Cary. I never let work stress me out."

He was about to ask if she ever took time off when the crowd around them grumbled again.

"Mr. Hudson! You're six feet two. Go play or move!" Kyle West called out from three rows up.

"Wish you cared as much about independent variables as this game, Kyle," Cary retorted. "You blew yesterday's quiz."

Kyle paled. "Don't tell my mom."

As the crowd around them laughed and a wad of paper flew toward the freckle-faced junior, Cary made his way down the stands. Catching Mrs. West's eye, he couldn't resist winking at her. "I'm guessing she already knows," he murmured, just as the referee called another time-out.

A WEEK LATER, MELISSA rapped two times on his door before barging in. "Uncle Cary? You home?"

Cary glanced at his watch. It was seven o'clock. Usually Melissa was either doing homework or talking on the phone at this time of night. "You okay?"

She shook her head. "No. I'm so glad you're home. Dad's working late and Brian's still at practice."

"What's wrong?" he asked, instantly

concerned. Melissa looked to be on the verge of tears.

"Come see my car," she said, her lip trembling. "Someone ruined all my tires! I don't know how it could have happened."

"Let's go see."

"It's bad," she said.

Grabbing a jacket and a cell phone, Cary followed her down his walkway and out to her trusty blue Civic, practically lying on the curb in front of her house, its tires completely flat. "Those tires are ruined all right."

As if relieved that he finally believed her, her light-blue eyes filled with tears. "I was about to go out when I found it like this!"

Though his knee-jerk reaction was to ask where she'd been headed, he focused on the car. "Did you drive through a new neighborhood or something?" he asked, even though he knew a few stray nails wouldn't cause this much damage.

"No, I drove straight home from school."

After checking the tires for nails or other debris, he finally saw a jagged cut near the rim of one. "These have been slashed."

"Dad's going to be so mad."

With his thumb, Cary wiped a tear from the corner of her eye. "No, he won't."

She hiccuped. "You think?"

"I know. He's my brother, remember? Have you called him yet?"

"Not yet."

Pointing to the cement curb bordering her lawn, he said, "Let's have a seat. Missy, I think we ought to call the police. Slashing tires is serious stuff, so we should report this. It could just be someone's idea of a prank, but we should be careful in any case."

Because she still looked worried she'd get in trouble, he added, "Your dad's going to want to contact the insurance agency, and they'll likely want the police to look at the damage, anyway." He wrapped an arm around her shoulder. "It's okay. Your dad will know this wasn't your fault."

Her cell phone rang. "Brian! Oh my goodness!" she said as soon as she clicked on in that dramatic way of hers that Cary knew so well. Cary stretched his legs as Melissa quickly summarized to her boyfriend what was happening.

A much calmer Melissa turned to him

after she clicked off. "Brian said you should call the police."

"I guess we'd better then," he said, his sarcasm completely wasted on his niece. Funny how teenagers never changed. Cary vividly remembered always putting his friends' advice in the forefront years ago, too.

After dialing Information, he called the police station. Recognizing the voice, he said, "Hey, Amanda, this is Cary Hudson. Any chance you could send Gary or Sam out this way? Melissa has a slight problem here." After telling her about the tires, he turned to his niece. "Someone will be here shortly."

Next he called his brother and filled him in. Luckily Dean was already on his way home.

Within minutes, a stream of cars approached.

Out of the first vehicle flew Brian, who rushed toward Melissa. Next came half the basketball team, three girls from Missy's cheer squad and assorted other seniors who were looking for a party.

Cary waved hello to everyone but stayed

seated. He'd known most of the kids for years and had taught nearly every one of them. They were good kids and were doing their best to give Melissa emotional support. Already his petite niece was standing a little straighter now that her hand was firmly encased in Brian's.

Finally a police cruiser appeared.

Cary stood motionless when he saw who'd come to help them out. Officer Gen Slate.

THE SCENE THAT greeted Gen was oddly familiar. Here in Lane's End—just as it had been in Beckley—everyone's business was cause for discussion. A whole crowd of kids gathered in front of a row of fifties-style ranch houses. Cary, a diminutive blonde and a really tall kid in sweats were in the middle of it all. Everyone looked to be talking at once.

Just as she was about to approach them, yet another car pulled up. An attractive man in a button-down shirt, jeans and the same dark-brown eyes as Cary's got out of his sedan. After hugging the girl, as well, he slapped the tall kid on the shoulder. Then, they all turned to Gen.

"Glad you're here, Officer," the man—likely Cary's brother considering the resemblance—said after examining the Civic. "Someone really did a number on my daughter's tires."

"It definitely looks that way," Gen said as she quickly jotted down a record of her first impressions. "Any idea why someone would deliberately do this?"

The girl glanced at her friends before turning to Gen. "No."

Just as Gen was wondering how to send the kids home without alienating the lot of them, Cary stepped forward.

"Guys, if you don't have information to contribute, you all better get on home."

"I'm not leaving," the tall kid—Brian—said.

"I can stay, too," a freckle-faced boy added, casting an almost wistful look toward Melissa.

Gen watched Cary's niece meet the boy's gaze before turning her head away, pink staining her cheeks.

"Go on home, Jimmy," Brian said. "Melissa's fine with me."

Jimmy shook his head. "Listen—"

Just as Gen was going to step in, Cary took control. "Brian, go ahead and stay. Melissa needs you. Everyone else, why don't you let Melissa call you later?"

Miraculously most of the kids listened and, with a few parting words to Melissa, went on their way.

Gen tapped her pen again. "Let's start from the top. I'll take your statements and some pictures. If I need anything else, I'll stop by tomorrow. It's getting late and I'm sure everyone's ready to go inside."

As Gen had hoped, her calm, direct manner soothed the girl's nerves. Melissa stepped away from Brian and answered Gen's questions, only pausing once or twice for her dad to add information.

There wasn't much to go on. Genevieve suspected Melissa's Civic was just a victim of a random prank, but she would look into it.

Within the hour, Brian went home, Melissa and her dad headed inside and Gen and Cary were left alone.

"Thanks for coming out," he said as she started toward her car. "Melissa was pretty upset."

"Don't thank me—it's my job," she quipped before she realized just how unfeeling she sounded.

His mouth tightened into a fine line. "Oh. Well. I guess it is."

"Well, um, like I said, I'll file this report and call back if I find out anything." She opened her car door, feeling stupid for being so uptight.

"Call Dean. He's her father."

"I…I was planning on it."

She was about to add more, anything to recreate the warmth in his gaze from the coffee shop. A howl directed her attention to Cary's fence, where a tricolor beagle, almost the exact replica of Sadie, watched them both.

She stepped forward. "Is that Sludge?"

After a second, Cary grinned. "Yep."

Sludge howled again.

Gen was charmed. Beagles, she could relate to. Approaching the fence, she held out her hand. "Hi, Sludge." When Sludge tilted his head to one side and watched her,

Gen knelt down, the edges of her long scarf grazing the grass below her.

Sludge eyed the wool with interest.

"I wouldn't—" Cary called out.

But it was too late.

In a lightning-fast move, Sludge chomped down on the wool and pulled hard.

Gen landed on the grass just as a good three-inch square was ingested by Sludge. "Sludge! Cary, my scarf—"

"Is ruined," Cary muttered in disapproval as Sludge chewed his prize without a bit of shame. "Sorry, he's a menace."

"He certainly is." Bending down to pet the dog, Gen scratched his ears. "Be careful, Sludge, or you're going to get my reputation for eating anything and everything that's unhealthy for you."

Cary's lips twitched before pointing to the frayed, wet wool she now held in her hand. "Sorry about your scarf."

"Don't worry about it," she said, wiping the grass from her thighs as she strode to her car. "Sadie's done crazy things, too."

"Thanks again for coming out."

"No problem. Remember, it's why I'm here." Gen tried to lighten her words with a smile, but neither came out the way she'd intended. Though she'd spoken the truth, she'd also been genuinely glad to try to help. "Please tell your brother I'll call him soon."

After a few parting words, Cary went inside and Gen got in her car.

As she backed out, she shook her head in dismay. Someone had slapped a Lion Pride sticker smack-dab in the middle of her rear windshield while she'd been taking Melissa's statement. Looked as though basketball fever was going to catch her whether she wanted to be caught or not.

CHAPTER FOUR

"It's CONTRACT DAY, Cary," Christy Pardue said from Cary's doorway. "As your department head, I've been informed to tell you to either sign the thing and turn it in or write a letter of resignation and let us hire someone else."

"Glad to feel so needed."

"Any time. It's why I get paid the big bucks."

Cary laughed. "So…I've got to make a decision, huh?"

"Yep. The school board is crunching numbers. Since Michael just announced he's leaving to take that job at Lakota, Evan's going crazy. He wants to know how many of us are coming back, pronto."

Looking at the contract that had been sitting in a folder on his desk for a month, he sighed. "Tell Evan he'll have my answer by two."

Christy's playful expression sobered. "You aren't really thinking of leaving, are you? You were going to help me teach that continuing-ed class this summer and give me a hand ordering new textbooks. You can't leave me with just Dave and Linda."

"Dave's easy and Linda is…okay."

"Linda's twenty-two years old—I could be her mother. Please sign your contract." Her eyes narrowed. "You *are* going to sign it, right?"

"I'll let you know by two."

Christy turned on her heel, leaving Cary to stare at his contract again.

Why was committing another three years such a big deal? He loved teaching at Lane's End. Surely he hadn't gotten so hurt by Kate that he was willing to change his whole life just to avoid her?

No, it was more than that.

Signing meant accepting how his life was. As long as he held off committing to the job, Cary could play with the idea of moving somewhere different, of *doing* something different.

Growing and changing. Taking a risk.

As Gen had said at the café, change was a good thing.

That stopped him in his tracks.

Now there was a person who obviously didn't mind starting over. She was as independent a woman as he'd ever come across, giving off "I'm self-sufficient" vibes like nobody's business. He admired her for that.

At the moment, he was stuck in Drive and his road was straight farm country. Nothing of interest for miles and miles. He'd taken it a hundred times.

But yet…

Closing his eyes, Cary thought of Dean and Melissa. The guys he went running with. Dave. Christy.

Lane's End. This was where he belonged. Cary knew it the way he knew Sludge would eat his Nikes if given the chance.

Deciding not to put the inevitable off a moment longer, Cary signed the contract and placed it in the folder to take down to the principal.

ON SATURDAY MORNING, Gen knew something had to be done. She'd tossed and turned all night, plagued by dreams of bas-

ketballs and lions and kids screaming like
banshees.

Her first thought when she awoke had
been about work. Again. Obviously she
needed some balance in her life, stat. But
how?

Padding to the bathroom, she flipped on
the light and grabbed her brush. As Gen
fixed her hair, she examined herself in the
mirror. She looked the same as ever. Boy-
ish figure. Lean and muscular, thanks to
the frequent workouts at the gym. Her long,
dark hair had always served her well. It was
easy to pull back and was her best feature,
in her opinion. Of course, not even really
good hair could keep a man's attention.

Thinking once again of her former partner, she wondered what had gone wrong.
Why weren't she and Keaton together, as
she'd hoped? Was it because she wasn't
girlie enough? Chatty enough? Interesting? They'd gotten along well and had been
good friends, but obviously he'd wanted
something—someone—else.

Remembering their frequent meals together, all she could remember Keaton
commenting on was her love of junk food.

That wasn't good. Maybe she'd been too aloof and afraid of showing him who she really was. She was already repeating that behavior with Cary, after all.

She remembered their meeting the other day. She hadn't felt so tongue-tied around a man since Keaton. Could she actually pursue another man after that fiasco? Did she even know how? Gen had to admit she'd never been good in the romance department.

Quickly she braided her hair, then padded into the kitchen, getting a bowl of Froot Loops as she poured another cup of coffee.

The only truly feminine person she knew was her sister. Margaret had also never been one to shy away from giving advice—and she'd had no trouble winning over her husband.

Before Gen chickened out, she picked up the phone and dialed.

"Hey, Genevieve! This is a surprise."

Gen was caught off guard by the exuberant greeting. "Hey, Meg. How are you?"

"I'm good. Oh—hold on a minute," she said as Gen heard cereal rattle on a tray.

"So did I surprise you, me knowing it was you right away? Shane got me caller ID."

Gen grinned. Some things made their way more slowly than others to Beckley, West Virginia. "I'm glad you finally have it. How are Will, Jackson and Emily?"

"Happy. Crying. Driving me crazy. The usual." Her tone turned thoughtful. "So why are you calling? Have you been injured again? Are you in the hospital?"

It was humbling to realize the only time she reached out to her family was on holidays or during medical emergencies. The last time Gen had called her sister out of the blue was after she'd sustained a knife wound during a gang altercation.

"I'm fine, Meg," she hastily replied. "Actually, I called because I need some advice."

"What's going on?"

Gen opened her mouth but couldn't say it. How could she admit to her beautiful, oh-so-together sister that she didn't know how to step out of her shell? "I need a hobby." She winced at the lame excuse for the call.

"Huh?"

"Okay. I know to a mother of three kids under five it sounds silly, but…got any ideas?"

"I thought you had that awful dog."

"Sadie's still around," Gen admitted, nodding to Sadie as she thumped her tail.

"And don't you work out like crazy?"

"Not as much as I used to. I was thinking I need some variety in my life. Maybe something a little more crafty." Gen closed her eyes as she heard what she was saying. Really, could she sound *any* more backward?

But Margaret wasn't laughing at all. "What? Like knitting? Crochet?"

Gen would rather stab someone with a knitting needle than try to figure out how to use one. "No."

"Hold on." Once again Gen heard her sister talking to all three kids, followed by another onslaught of cereal being poured. "I'm not fooled by this hobby talk for a second, Genevieve Slate. What's really going on?"

It was scary how Margaret could sound just like their mother. "Nothing."

"It is so something. It's a man. Right?"

It was more like a lack of one. But who was she to split hairs? "Kind of."

"Gen…just tell me."

"This morning it occurred to me that all I've been doing is working and taking care of Sadie. Maybe I need something to get me out more, give myself a reason to put on some lipstick and just relax once in a while."

"I get it."

"I doubt it. I don't think you've ever had to worry about being seen as just a friend by any guy." Although Gen said this with horror, she had always been impressed— and a bit jealous—that boys had always loved Margaret.

"Stop that talk," Margaret admonished. "Momma never gave you credit, Gen. Just because you weren't interested in prom dresses or lip gloss didn't mean you weren't attractive. You are, you know. You're beautiful."

Margaret's words were like a soothing balm, coating over a lifetime of old hurts and imagined slights. Once again Gen wondered if maybe the world hadn't pushed her away as much as she'd been pushing.

After her sister settled yet another argument with her children, she came back on the line. "Gen, I've got the perfect hobby. It's not quite crafty, but it's more your speed. Gardening."

Didn't that involve plants? Keeping things alive? "Seriously?"

"Gardening would be perfect. It's physical and you'll get to sweat. I know how you like to do that," she teased.

Now wait a minute! "Margaret—"

But all her sister did was speak a little louder. "You'll get to *nurture* something. Be outside. Be around other people."

"I'm around a lot of people with my job."

"Giving them tickets! That'll make you a lot of friends! Gardening is different. It's calm."

Calm did sound good. "How is gardening going to improve my love life?"

"Everyone who gardens talks about gardening. Maybe you could join a club," Margaret continued. The way she was rushing her words told Gen she was getting more and more excited by the suggestion.

"I'll keep that in mind," she said sarcastically.

As the kids started going crazy in the background, Margaret said, "Ugh, these three are driving me batty today. I've gotta go. Did I help at all?"

She sounded so enthusiastic Gen couldn't say no. Although Gen wasn't great at asking Meg for help, she wanted a better relationship with her sister. Perhaps the gap wasn't quite as one-sided as Gen had always thought it to be and Meg had just been waiting for Gen to make the first step. Maybe—just maybe—one day they could be a whole lot closer. "Some," she said.

"Easter's coming. Grow a lily. It might be fun."

One plant. She could do that. "Maybe I will. Oh! I almost forgot to tell you—I won't be coming home for Easter. I've gotta work."

"I kinda figured that since you've never been able to make it home for many holidays." Will, Meg's baby, was now crying hard enough to wake the dead. "Sorry. I really gotta go. Bye!"

After Gen hung up, she turned to Sadie. "I have a plan. One day soon I'm going to grow lilies and think about something else besides work, Cary Hudson or industrial-size bags of peanut M&M's."

Sadie rolled to her side and groaned just as Gen's cell phone rang. "Slate."

"Gen, I've got a problem," Sam said. "I can't find the report about Mrs. Bodwell's car break-in. Any idea where you put it?"

"Yep." As Gen told Sam where she filed her paperwork before going off duty, then volunteered to help him find it, Sadie opened one eye and blinked.

Gen had a pretty good idea what the beagle was thinking. Her new hobby might not come about quite as quickly as she hoped.

"I'M ON TRAFFIC DUTY?" Gen asked late Monday afternoon. "*Again?* It's raining." Directing traffic in the rain meant wet feet and annoyed drivers. She'd be soaked to the skin in minutes.

Gen didn't really mind the duty, but since she'd been asked to direct traffic the last two times it rained, the assignment felt like a game of "let's haze the rookie."

She'd already gone through this ritual with the Cincinnati Police Department and she wasn't eager to do it again. "Who decided the new girl needed this job?" she said out loud to the nearly empty rec room.

"This old guy," Sergeant John Conrad called from the far corner, and her heart jumped into her throat. "I thought you could take a shift," he said in his trademark scratchy voice. "You know, do your part?" As he stepped out of the shadows, he added, "Unless you got a problem with that, Slate?"

She stood at attention. "No, sir. I have no problem with the assignment. I'm sorry. I didn't see you over by the coffeemaker."

"I figured as much." Sergeant Conrad grinned, causing the creases around his eyes to deepen. "At ease, Gen."

She attempted to backtrack. "I didn't mean to complain. It was more like good-natured griping."

"I hear ya. I do the same thing about the bran flakes my wife makes me eat every morning." He cleared his throat. "Since we're chatting and all, the lieutenant asked me to check in with you." Conrad sat down, gingerly resting his back against the back of the plastic chair. "So, you, uh, doing okay in Lane's End? Getting used to the place? Getting used to the department?"

"I am." Gen sat down across from him, noticing Sam Clark sitting nearby reading a magazine.

"Good. Good. Things are different here than in the CPD. Our community expects you to take time to get to know them." Tapping a beat-up ballpoint pen on his clipboard, he added, "It makes your job easier, by the way, if you're familiar with everyone."

Gen knew what he was trying to say. It had been hard to get used to the new department's way of doing things. In Lane's End, the cops worked together, not competitively as they had in Cincinnati.

Gen had also been trying to choose her words more carefully, since she'd been fool enough to let all the cops in her old department witness her jealousy of Keaton's new girlfriend. But as Gen realized she'd just been openly complaining about traffic duty, she knew she needed to work on that.

"I did go to a basketball game," she said, eager to at least prove that she'd been trying to get out in the community more.

Sam snorted from his seat, showing he wasn't that engrossed in his reading, after all—and reminded Gen that she'd fought the excursion to the school last week tooth and nail.

Sergeant Conrad nodded. "That's the way. I thought I'd heard you went to the Lions game the other night. I missed it—grandkids."

"It's too bad you didn't make it." As she recalled the way the Lions had fought after slipping by six points, she added, "It was pretty exciting. Half the town was there." Including Cary Hudson.

"Lieutenant Banks recommended we assign additional officers for the next game. If the Lions keep winning, things could get out of hand."

Recalling how loud and vibrant the place had been, Gen attempted to imagine it even more jam-packed.

"I heard through the grapevine that the high school wants to do a parade if we go to state," Sam interjected, his magazine now closed.

"That'll be fun," the sergeant said, sarcasm coating his voice. "A third of the town's going to be in the parade, another third is going to want to watch the thing and the last third is going to raise enough Cain about the traffic and congestion that we'll wish the game of basketball had never been invented."

Gen laughed. After getting caught up in downtown's traffic, she had a feeling she knew which third she would be a part of.

The sergeant tapped his watch. "Speaking of traffic, half of Lane's End is going to be heading through downtown right about now. If you haven't figured it out yet, families here take their soccer practices seriously."

"Even in the rain?"

"Especially in the rain. Better get a move on, Slate. And don't forget your slicker."

"I won't."

She darted a look toward Sam as she exited the room. As if lying in wait, he brushed at the perfect crease along the sleeve of his crisp oxford. "Shame about the rain, Gen," he said. "It's not supposed to let up before nightfall."

"Thanks for the update."

Hastily Gen grabbed a headset, pulled

out a bright yellow slicker from her locker, then strode to her cruiser. Thank goodness she'd already inspected the car when she'd come on shift so she wouldn't have to do the lengthy once-over in the rain. Finally she radioed that she was leaving the premises and pulled out of the parking lot.

Today's assignment was yet another taste of life as a small-town cop. Every day involved doing whatever was necessary to maintain peace and tranquility in town and chipping in as a team to do just that. Being a team player was a hard way to go in one respect since she was so used to trying to prove herself and competing for recognition.

But as she parked the car in the main intersection, donned the rain gear and stepped out into the drizzle, she felt the weighty responsibility she'd always carried with pride. Someone needed to do the jobs others didn't want to. Someone needed to step up and take responsibility.

And though she might complain about getting wet, she'd never been one to dodge duty.

CHAPTER FIVE

As SERGEANT CONRAD had predicted, the traffic was heavy. With practiced ease, Gen motioned cars through the intersection, giving grumblers her best stony glare and nodding her thanks to friendlier drivers. To Gen's surprise, two high school kids even smiled shyly when she waved them on through.

Despite her concerns about the rain, the slicker had kept Gen relatively dry. She just wished it were summer—the damp chill kept the job from being completely bearable.

After her shift, Gen clocked out and raced home to her rooms on the top floor of a sixty-year-old white clapboard house at the corner of Plymouth and Third Avenue. Consisting of a bedroom, small bath, galley kitchen and comfortable living area, the place had more than enough space for her and Sadie.

The old oak floors and thick rag rugs her landlady had made years ago made Gen smile, and suited her low-maintenance lifestyle to a T. Sadie barked a greeting from her kennel the minute Gen opened the front door.

"Hey, girl," Gen said as she placed her purse on the kitchen table. "Let's get you some fresh air." Sadie whined as Gen clipped on her leash and led her outside.

As expected, the dog balked about doing her business in the rain, but Gen wouldn't take no for an answer. She was glad she still had her slicker on as the dog combed the perimeter.

"Hi, Gen!" Bonnie Walker, her landlady, shouted from the back porch. "You picking up after that dog?"

"Yes, ma'am."

As Sadie trotted back and forth, smelling every bush in sight, Bonnie called out again. "It's taking Sadie a while."

"It always does."

As Sadie inspected a tree, seeming to forget all about her disdain for rain, Bonnie pointed to Gen's hair. "You're getting soaked."

Her landlady had a flair for the obvious. "Yes, ma'am."

"When Sadie's done, come on in and have some cookies. I'll make a fresh pot of coffee, too."

The hot liquid sounded heavenly, but she was a mess, and Bonnie was a meticulous housekeeper. There was no way Gen wanted to offend her by dripping water on her rugs. "Thanks, but maybe some other time."

"No, you don't. You take off your rain gear and join me in the kitchen."

Even Sadie's ears looked muddy. "Sadie—"

"She's just a bit wet. Come on in and I'll pull out a towel for her." Bonnie paused. "Truth is, I could sure use some company."

Gen couldn't refuse that. "I'll be right there."

As soon as Sadie was finished, Gen dutifully led her to Bonnie's back door, wiped down her paws, then slipped out of her own dripping slicker and shoes. Immediately a curtain of warmth enveloped her.

Though Bonnie was old enough to be her

mother, she always made Gen feel comfortable, thanks to her frank way of speaking and easy smiles.

"So tell me how your day directing traffic went," Bonnie said as she placed two mugs of piping-hot coffee and a plate of chocolate-chip cookies on the table.

"It was about what you'd expect—wet and long." Realizing even she hadn't known she was going to be out in the rain until a few hours ago, Gen stared at Bonnie. "How did you know what I was doing today?"

"Two women from church saw you on their way to visit me. They said you did a good job, like a real pro." Bonnie cackled. "They said you were giving a couple of dads in minivans a good dressing-down when they tried to cut off the other drivers. How'd you learn to do all those hand gestures and such?"

"My ex-partner taught me," Gen said aloud, recalling Keaton's advice. "Directing traffic's no fun in the rain, but it's not hard. Just takes some getting used to."

Bonnie nodded sagely. "Like arthritis.

My hands certainly aren't what they used to be."

Gen glanced at Bonnie's hand, saw her swollen knuckles and how the fingers were bent at uncomfortable angles. "Ouch."

"I'm okay. I could take more medicine, but it makes me sleepy." She pushed the plate closer to Gen. "Have another cookie."

Gen couldn't refuse, especially since Bonnie had put out a rawhide chew for Sadie and it was clear her dog wasn't planning to leave anytime soon. "Thank you."

Gen stayed with Bonnie a full hour before saying goodbye. Bonnie looked tired and Gen had things to do, not to mention that no amount of rawhide would hold over Sadie at dinnertime.

Once at home, she turned on the stereo and poured a generous amount of Mighty Munchies for Sadie. Although she was now dry, Gen took a hot shower, but not before popping a frozen pizza into the oven for herself.

Finally settled, Gen leaned back on the couch, work crossing her mind once again. Who had damaged Melissa Hudson's car?

Though she'd spoken to Dean on the

phone earlier this morning, Gen had decided to go ahead and meet with Melissa again anyway. While her gut told her the vandal had randomly chosen Melissa's Civic, experience said it was better to be a little overzealous than remiss, especially since she was new to Lane's End. The townspeople would want to know what had happened so the culprit could be punished.

For an instant she considered talking to Sam, to see how he would recommend handling the case, then rejected that idea. She'd only look weak if she asked for help. And while she might admit her personal faults to her sister, admitting professional ones would never do, especially if she wanted to fit in and be accepted.

CARY DRUMMED HIS fingers on his binder while Evan droned on about the state of Ohio's new graduation requirements. Usually Cary enjoyed the opportunity to see his coworkers and interact with other adults for an hour, but today's topic was beyond boring. It also didn't help that he could see Kate every time he looked at Evan, reminding Cary once again that he'd been the proverbial fool in love. To avoid catching Kate's eye, he stared at his binder.

Christy, on the other hand, relieved her boredom by passing notes just like the kids in his class.

Kate's now seeing Andrew Richards's dad. What do you think of that?

Cary fought to keep his expression neutral. That was news. Through the grapevine, he'd heard Michael had dropped Kate as soon as he'd accepted Lakota's offer. Discovering Kate had already moved on was a true surprise. Especially when her new "someone" was as fake as city councilman Clay Richards.

Kate was obviously putting her cool blond charm to good use. How could Cary have been so gullible to think that she'd been in love with him?

Maybe she'll become a lady of leisure soon, he wrote back. He winked when Christy opened the note and grinned.

"Hudson, you have a question about our topic?"

Busted. "No, Evan," he said.

"No questions about the new credit requirements?"

"No. I've read the information carefully. But I'll do it again just to make sure I haven't missed something," he said, deliberately ignoring Dave's laugh, which he hadn't quite hidden behind his cough.

"Good." Evan stepped from behind the podium. "Before we wrap up, we couldn't end this staff meeting without acknowledging Brad. As everyone knows, Coach Jackson has done a tremendous job this season. Because tomorrow night's game is crucial, on Wednesday we'll be going to our short schedule and hosting a pep rally at one o'clock. Tickets for the game will go on sale at lunch."

Spontaneous applause broke out for the likable basketball coach.

Evan tapped the podium. "First bell rings in four minutes. Have a good day."

Echoing their students' enthusiasm at the end of class, the teachers eagerly filed out of the staff room. In the commotion, Cary bumped into Kate. "Sorry," he said, his voice catching in his throat.

"No problem." Resting her silvery-blue eyes on him in a way that used to make his pulse race a little quicker, she said softly, "How are you, Cary?"

What could he say with a crowd of interested onlookers around? "Fine. Great."

"That's good." Tilting her head to meet his gaze, she added, "I haven't seen you much in our neck of the woods."

There was no way he was going anywhere near the foreign-language department if he could help it. "I've been busy."

"I…yes." She smiled, showing beautiful teeth. "See you."

"Yeah."

"See you," Christy mocked in a whisper as she walked beside him. "She has such nerve."

Cary privately agreed, though he didn't say so as they took the steps into the school basement, affectionately known as "the catacombs" by the staff.

He was just about to step into his classroom when the students came roaring in, Melissa being one of them. Holding her cell phone, she rushed to his side. "I just talked to Dad. That policewoman is coming by tonight to talk to me again, but Dad's supposed to take some clients out to dinner. Can you be there?"

"What time?"

"Five-thirty."

Mentally Cary juggled his schedule. "Sure I can, sweetheart. Don't worry."

"I wonder why she's coming back. Do you think she's going to blame me for what happened to my tires? She's asking a lot of questions. Talking to everybody! Brian said she spoke to his parents."

He squeezed her shoulder. "I'm sure she was just doing her job when she talked to Mr. and Mrs. McCullough. Go on now or you'll be late for class."

Uncharacteristically, Melissa hugged him before darting away. "Thanks!"

"Anytime," he said just as his first period students rolled in, most still looking half-asleep.

After asking them to pull out their homework, Cary thought of Gen Slate and wondered what she'd learned about the vandalism. And he wondered why he was so eager to see her again. She'd been almost all business when she'd investigated the damage to Melissa's car. Maybe he'd only imagined there was something special between them.

Again.

Hadn't he learned a thing from Kate?

CHAPTER SIX

TWO RAPS ON Cary's door announced Officer Genevieve Slate's arrival.

"Melissa called and asked that I meet you here instead of at her house," Gen said as soon as he greeted her.

"Yep. Dean's got clients in town tonight, so she's staying with me. Come on in. Melissa, as usual, is running about ten minutes late. She should be here any minute."

"No problem."

After Cary closed the door, he guided her inside. "How are you?" he asked.

"I'm good." With a shrug she added, "Working hard."

Gesturing to her uniform, he said, "Looks like it." Gen filled out the utilitarian slacks and blouse pretty nicely.

As they walked to the couch in the center of the room, Cary caught a whiff of perfume. The light, fresh scent caught his senses and held on tight.

He was so attracted to her. For a split second Cary imagined Gen at his home more often, hanging out in old jeans, watching football or one of those old movies she mentioned she loved so much.

The vision caught him off guard, making him antsy. "Would you like a soda or something?"

"Thanks, but I'm fine for now. Pretty place," she said.

Cary looked around the room, attempting to see it from her eyes. "The rooms are narrow, and the ceiling is almost too low for me, but it feels right, you know?"

She pointed to the far wall, where his collection of old tin signs hung in a scattered fashion. "Tell me about those."

"I started collecting them about ten years ago." Pointing to the large, mustard-colored rectangle advertising Johnson's Chewing Tobacco, he said, "I saw that in Lebanon and couldn't resist it. Next thing I knew I was buying a couple more, sanding them down and fixing them up."

"They look great."

"Thanks. I was never into fancy artwork, so these are more my style."

"Mine, too," she whispered.

There was that connection again. "As I said, Melissa should be here in a second," he continued, doing his best to fill the silence.

"It's no problem. I've got some time." She pulled out her notepad and pencil. "Hey, I just noticed it's suspiciously quiet around here. Where's Sludge?"

"In the backyard. I'm surprised he didn't howl a greeting when you walked up the drive."

"I was actually prepared to see him." She fingered the plain blue collar of her shirt. "See, no scarf today."

He laughed, glad their conversation was once again as easy as it had been at the Corner Café. "So how was your day?"

"Nuts. A couple of things came up after I made plans to come over here. Now I've got to return to the station, type up three reports and return a few phone calls."

Her mention of work made him remember her reason for visiting. "Melissa said you have some more questions for her? Why?"

"No specific reason. I'm just following standard procedure."

Cary didn't buy that for a second. Gen didn't seem the type to put off stacks of reports just to follow the rules.

Before he could question her reasoning, the back door slammed. "Uncle Cary, Sludge almost attacked me when I walked through the back door. I swear, he almost ate my—oh."

Gen stood up. "Hi, there, Melissa."

"Hi." As she stepped closer to Cary, Gen couldn't help but admire the girl's outfit. Dressed in a snug designer T-shirt and low-riding jeans, Melissa looked as if she'd stepped out of one of the trendy teen-store catalogues. Her thick blond hair was pulled up in a messy knot, the kind young girls could pull off in a second, but older women tried for hours to emulate.

After they all sat down, Melissa looked at Gen's notebook as if it were about to erupt into flames any second.

Gen cleared her throat. "Melissa, I'm just looking for a bit more information on the night of the incident, okay? Since it's not clear whether someone wanted to slash your tires specifically or if this person randomly chose your car, I think we should further investigate who might want to do such a thing."

"I already told you I don't know."

"Melissa—"

"It's okay," Gen interrupted, seeing that Cary was about to reprimand Melissa for being snippy. The girl's obstinate tone felt familiar to Gen. She didn't like being pressed for information, either. But the cop in her knew that more questions needed to be asked. "I know this is frustrating, but I'm on your side. Is there anything you can think of that might help?" she asked, her voice gentle. "There might be something new you remember since that night. Let's start at the beginning."

Melissa groaned. "But—"

Gen looked directly at Melissa. "Please?"

Melissa slumped. "All right."

"You sure you don't want anything to drink, Gen?" Cary said.

"Actually, I think I will have a glass of water," she said, catching his eye. The look that passed between them showed that they were both on the same page. This was fixing to be a long meeting.

As Melissa answered questions, Gen tried to pretend that this was just a usual interview. From the moment she'd seen Cary again she'd felt that same pull toward him that she'd felt every other time they'd come in contact. He was attractive. And…nice.

When he'd asked her how she was, Gen had been tempted to tell him about her conversation with Margaret, how Bonnie had given her cookies. How things were going better at the station now that she'd decided to let down her guard a little bit.

But all that seemed too weird. What if he was merely being friendly and thought she was coming on too strong?

Belatedly Gen realized Cary and Melissa were waiting for her to speak. Gen cleared her throat. "Melissa, perhaps you could tell me what you do on a usual day. Who are your friends?"

"Well, first, I'm up every morning at five to get ready for school. Then I leave the house by six-forty."

"Do you pick up anyone on the way to school?"

"No, my dad won't let me. He says cars full of teenagers can be dangerous."

"He's right. So you never give anyone a ride?"

"Nope. Well, the only time I've done it is when Amy Blythe missed the bus last Monday and she needed a ride." Meeting Cary's gaze, she rolled her eyes. "That was a disaster."

"Why?"

Melissa grimaced. "My dad made me pick her up."

"Amy's a bit of a loner so doesn't have a lot of friends," Cary interjected. "Dean and I have asked Melissa to be nice to her."

"I *was* nice, but Amy kept wanting to listen to some lousy music station. When I told her to leave my stereo alone, she got all bent out of shape. Once we got to school, she practically broke my car door slamming it shut."

As she glared at her uncle, Melissa sniffed. "I still don't understand why you were so mad about that."

"Because I think you could have tried to

be more patient, tried to get to know Amy instead of putting down her taste in music. She needs a friend, Melissa."

"That's not fair," Melissa retorted. "I don't see why I need to be her friend when she's the one who's so difficult. I have a lot of friends already."

"You could always use another, right?"

"Not her. She's impossible. She's different, Uncle Cary."

Gen's pencil paused. Melissa's statement brought back memories of being different, as well, though she'd had her share of friends. Gen couldn't help but admire Cary's efforts to include Amy. Though Gen honestly didn't think it would make much of a difference, she respected that he was hoping Melissa would accept Amy's differences instead of try to change the girl.

Wouldn't it have been something if Gen's mother had done that a little more often?

Continuing with her story, Melissa said, "You chewed me out in front of everyone, too."

"I don't think it was 'everyone,' and all I said was you were lucky to have a car to drive as well as that expensive stereo. Not every girl your age can say the same."

Gen jumped in before Melissa could say another word. "Okay, this information could be helpful." She jotted a small note about Amy in her book. "Now I seem to remember Brian McCullough. He's your boyfriend, right?"

"Right," Melissa replied, her expression going soft.

"Pretty serious?" She directed that question to Cary, who shrugged. Clearly he wasn't all that comfortable discussing his niece's love life.

"Oh, yes," Melissa interrupted, not appreciating Gen asking Cary's opinion of her relationship. "We've been going out for six months." Judging by Melissa's smile, Gen guessed the relationship was going well.

"Did you date anyone before?" Gen asked, writing down Brian's name.

"No one seriously."

Gen struggled, wondering how much to push. "Anyone more serious than others?"

"I don't think so," Melissa said, shrugging.

"There was Jimmy Aiken," Cary interjected. "Even if you weren't serious, he was." He gave Gen a look that told her he didn't particularly like Jimmy.

"Who's Jimmy?" Gen asked, vaguely recalling the name.

"He plays basketball, too, but he's not a starter like Brian. He and I only went out twice." She wrinkled her nose. "He gave me a card and said he loved me."

"He's had a crush on Melissa for some time," Cary added. "He was here the night we called you."

Recalling the boy with freckles, Gen made note of that.

They talked some more. Gen learned about cheerleading, about Melissa's other clubs and organizations, but nothing of importance. Nothing and no one jumped out or sounded suspicious.

Realizing she wasn't going to get much else out of Melissa, Gen closed her notebook. "Well, I guess that's everything I need. Thanks for your time."

Melissa hopped up. "Can I go now, Uncle Cary? Brian's got practice and I want to go watch."

"What about dinner?"

"I'll grab something on the way to school."

"What? Chips and a Coke like you did last night?"

"I'll bring Brian back here after practice for soup and sandwiches."

"Okay."

Gen bit her lip to keep from smiling. Not only were the teenager's eating habits extremely familiar, she also spoke to Cary just as Gen had spoken to her own dad years ago, in perfect teen give-and-take. Gen was impressed by Cary's ease with it.

"Be back by eight. After you two eat, Brian can go on home and you can do your homework."

"But—"

"Is your project done for World History?"

She dropped her chin. "No."

"Then you have quite a bit of work to do."

"But, Dad—"

"Is busy working. You're stuck with me. So it's eight o'clock or nothing—take it or leave it. Besides, you've got to be at the game tomorrow night, right?"

Melissa brightened. "You're right! I forgot!"

"So you'll get to see Brian at school and at the game tomorrow, okay?"

As Gen watched the teenager scamper out, her phone already attached to her ear, she released a sigh. "Wow."

Cary laughed. "Yeah. She's always been like that—in a hurry."

"You're good with her."

For a moment Cary looked surprised, then he chuckled softly. "I should be. I've helped take care of her since she was four."

"Sam said you moved next door to Dean years ago."

"I did. My brother's wife, Valerie, took off when Melissa was just three, and Dean needed all the support he could get. It seemed like fate when this house came on the market around the same time."

Gen could only imagine the toll Valerie's leaving had had on both Cary and Dean, let alone a young child. "That had to be an incredibly difficult time for you all."

"You could say that. None of us imagined that Valerie would actually leave.

What kind of woman abandons her daughter?"

"I don't know. Did Valerie ever explain why she left?"

"More or less. She and Dean got married young, just months after they met. They seemed happy until Melissa was born. Then I think Valerie just snapped. Dean came home one day to find her waiting for him, saying that she couldn't handle their life. She didn't want the responsibility of a child, didn't want to be married. It crushed my brother."

"Does Melissa ever hear from her mom?"

"Not too much. I don't know the specifics, but Dean laid down the law with Valerie when she showed up a few years later wanting to see how Melissa was."

Gen knew what she would have said to that. "Too little, too late."

"Exactly," Cary said with a grin. "Dean told Valerie that he would never put Melissa through the hurt of being abandoned by her mom again. He would only allow contact if Valerie wanted to see her on a regular basis."

"Let me guess—she took off." Gen could

only imagine how hard that must have been for the Hudsons.

"Yep. I think she sends birthday and Christmas cards but not much else."

Steepling his fingers, Cary looked squarely at Gen. "Valerie's behavior threw us all for a loop. Dean started spending more time at work to support Melissa and him and, I think, to distance himself from what happened. Melissa had to go through a couple of years of counseling when she was around twelve. For a while, she blamed Valerie's departure on herself."

"Poor thing."

"Yeah. Dean actually ended up letting Melissa call Valerie not too long ago. Luckily for everyone, Dean's ex-wife had matured enough to be pretty forthright about her faults. I think that conversation healed a lot of hurts."

"Your brother seems to be a good man."

"He is. We're different in a lot of ways. He's always been a little more driven, more aloof. Valerie was a beautiful woman, and I know when Dean got married he felt he'd done everything right. It's too bad it took her leaving to make him realize that rarely does anything ever go 'right.' He's only begun to date again in the past couple of years."

A dog's howl saved Gen from attempting to say anything to that. Inside, she was caught between marveling at how well Cary knew his brother, and imagining what it must have been like for this tight-knit family to go through so much heartache.

"I knew Sludge wouldn't be quiet for long," Cary said, lightening the atmosphere. "Let me go get him." With a wink, he said, "Keep your shoes on."

"I bet you say that to all the girls."

Cary laughed. "Hold on." He rose and walked to the back of the living room, where Gen assumed the kitchen was.

Within seconds Sludge came roaring in. Gen patiently stood still while the beagle boldly sniffed her ankles.

"Sludge, sit down."

Amazingly the dog sat, though the look in his dark-brown eyes showed that he wasn't happy about minding. Gen once again compared Sludge to her own Sadie. While both were tricolor, Sludge's colors leaned toward black while Sadie's spots were mainly brown.

Sludge also held a note of mischief in his eyes, making him look like a practical joker.

Now that he wasn't eating her scarf, Gen was charmed. Reaching out, she placed her fingers near his nose. He sniffed twice before treating her to a giant lick.

"We're in luck. Sludge hasn't looked at your shoes once."

"He must know better than to mess with regulation leather," Gen teased.

"He always has been a little wary of authority." Gesturing toward the kitchen, Cary said, "Would you like another glass of water? Cup of coffee?"

"No. I'd better get going," Gen said, tamping down the regret she felt. Warring emotions coursed through her, making her think of how much she'd love to relax on Cary's couch. Find out if those shoulders and arms really were as firm and sculpted as she guessed. Wear her hair down…attempt to flirt a little. See where this attraction to him could go.

But duty called. "I really do have to return some phone calls."

He stepped back. "Right. I'd almost forgotten. Phone calls and reports."

"Yep. Always paperwork," she added in a rush, saying the truth but wishing for something different.

"I won't keep you then." Cary walked to the door. Sludge followed, his tail wagging as he walked.

Gen patted the dog's head and decided to take a chance. "So—are you going to the game tomorrow night?" She held up a hand to stop his reply. "Scratch that. Of course you are. What I was going to say was, I'm going, too, and—" she took a deep breath and a giant leap "—I wondered if maybe you wanted to go together."

Mischief and warmth blended together in Cary's eyes. "Are you asking me out, Gen?"

Oh, no, she'd read him wrong. "Maybe," she said, hesitation in her voice. As much as she wanted to make more friends and be more outgoing, she couldn't survive another Keaton situation.

"Yes."

"Yes?" Had she heard him correctly?

"I'll pick you up."

"If you want. Or I could just meet you there."

"Not a chance. How about we go out to eat first? Do you eat Mexican?"

"I can eat anything." When Cary chuckled, Gen said, "I mean, I love Mexican food." What was happening to her? You'd think she'd never planned a date with a man before!

"How about I pick you up around five-thirty or six o'clock? The game starts at seven-thirty."

"My shift ends tomorrow at four, so that would be fine."

"Great. Where do you live?"

Hastily she pulled out a card and wrote her home address on the back. When Sludge came closer, nudging her jacket as if it were a tasty appetizer, Gen darted for the door. "I'll see you then."

"Okay."

"And I'll call you if I get a lead on the person who damaged Melissa's car."

"I hope you call soon, no matter what." The look in his eyes dissolved Gen's doubts about his feelings. Before she knew it, she was back in her cruiser, feeling more feminine in a starched blue uniform and polyester pants than she ever had before.

What was it about Cary Hudson that made the simplest things sound appealing?

Suddenly her radio squawked, effectively ending all daydreams. "Slate? We got an altercation at 1633 Cheyenne. Copy?"

"I'm on it. Five minutes, tops."

Amanda chuckled. "Take your time. It's only Mrs. Fogle. She and her daughter are at it again."

"I copy that." Carefully Gen drove away from Cary's house, stopping only to wave at a curly-headed blonde about Melissa's age watching from her front steps across the street.

CHAPTER SEVEN

"NO, MOM. I didn't mean that," Gen said, trying in vain to keep her voice even and calm. It wasn't going too well.

Especially since her mother wasn't making their conversation an easy one.

Wearily, Gen reflected on her earlier chat with Margaret and was twice as glad she'd chosen to give her sister a call. It had felt good to speak to Meg one-on-one, without their mom changing little details in the translation.

Obviously frustrated, her mother's voice rose sharply. "What *did* you mean, Genevieve? When Margaret told me you weren't coming home for Easter I was sure I had misunderstood. And now when I ask you what is more important than family on such a special holiday, you talk to me about work? I'm very disappointed."

Nobody could lay on the guilt trip like

her mother. And nobody else could make her feel like an awkward twelve-year-old in the space of five minutes. "Momma, I'm new here. Since I'm the newest on the force, I have to stay." Gen took a deep, cleansing breath.

"You are not new. You've been putting your life in danger for years."

Gen didn't dare touch the life-in-danger jab. "Momma, here in Lane's End I am the new girl. New girls work holidays." Against her will, she cringed at her words. She would've given anyone else what-for if they'd even thought of referring to her as a girl, but if the excuse appeased her mother, she'd learn to live with the name.

"You should have told them you had plans."

"How could I? Everyone knows I don't have family nearby."

"Yes, you do, young lady. And we're right here in Beckley, waiting for you to remember."

Gen winced. "Momma, I meant I'm single." Trying again, she said, "Come now, you know I'm right. I should be working instead of someone who has a spouse or children."

"That should be you, too. You need to settle down like your sister."

Gen had heard those words a hundred times. But after hearing how busy Margaret had been when they'd talked just days before, Gen didn't feel quite so stung by her mother's comment. Maybe Meg's life wasn't always perfect, either.

"Genevieve? Did you hear me?"

Probably the whole town of Beckley had! "Yes, ma'am."

"Are you being cheeky?"

"No, Momma." She had to get off the phone. Had to before she broke the receiver from gripping it so hard. "I've gotta go."

"Why?"

"I'm going to a basketball game. Basketball's a pretty big deal around here. The high school team's doing a real good job." Gen closed her eyes in frustration.

"Who's taking you?" In a far more syrupy voice, her mother asked, "Do you have a date?"

The doorbell rang. "Yes."

"Well, my goodness, Genevieve, do tell. What kind of man—"

"He's at the door, and I shouldn't keep him waiting. I've gotta go, Momma. Love you. Bye."

Gen clicked off, ran to catch the door and opened it with a flourish. "Hi."

"Hi, yourself," Cary said with a grin. "I didn't realize you were living at Bonnie's place." As he took a quick look around the second-floor apartment, Gen was glad she hadn't hesitated to rent it when Bonnie had given her a tour. "What's it like living above her?"

"Good. Why do you ask?"

"No reason. It's just that she can be a little…eccentric."

Thinking of her conversation with her mother, Gen laughed. "I can be that way, too." Remembering their first chat about Lion pride, Gen held out her arms to showcase her gold-and-black outfit. "So what do you think? Am I spirited enough?"

Cary skimmed his eyes over her black jeans, black T-shirt and gold scarf looped around her neck. "I think you look great," he said with a slow smile. "I like those jeans."

They were a little more formfitting than the Levi's she normally wore. Gen was glad she'd taken the time to look a bit more feminine. "Thanks," she said simply, suddenly at a loss for what else to say. Good grief, was she blushing?

Quickly she grabbed her purse, closed the door behind her, then turned the bolt. "I'm ready."

"Come on, then. I'm about to introduce you to some of the best Mexican food in Ohio."

HOURS LATER, GEN decided that their evening had been just about perfect. Cary was easy to talk to, and his laid-back nature enabled Gen to at least pretend she could be that way, too.

Their dinner had been good, the restaurant noisy and crowded. Nearly half the patrons knew Cary and weren't the least bit shy about walking over to their table to say hello.

Gen valiantly attempted to remember names, which was getting simpler since she saw more than a couple of familiar faces. Sam was there with Meagan. So was Cary's brother, Dean. Gen couldn't get over the resemblance between them and could tell they were close.

High school kids were crammed into too-small booths. Their raucous laughter encouraged everyone else in the place to speak loudly, too.

The enthusiasm evident at the restaurant had been a good warm-up for the game. As expected, still more familiar faces greeted Gen when she and Cary entered the gymnasium. Sergeant Conrad was on duty and waved them in. For nearly two hours Gen sat next to Cary as Melissa and her fellow cheerleaders jumped and cheered the Lions on to a historic victory.

When the final buzzer sounded and the whole gymnasium erupted into triumphant screams, Gen found herself singing the school's fight song with everyone else.

It was only when they were alone again in Cary's Explorer that she struggled for something to say.

"I'm glad you asked me to the game," he said. "This was a lot of fun."

Gen liked how much of a gentleman he was. While it was true that she'd asked him out, he'd been the one to make their date such a success. "I'm so glad they won."

"Me, too. Tomorrow would have been horrible if they'd lost. I think I teach half the basketball team, and the rest of the students would have been devastated. Not to mention the whole town!"

Gen laughed. "I never thought about those consequences."

"I can't help but think about them." Reaching out, he took her hand. "Even if they'd lost, I wouldn't regret this evening. You, Gen Slate, are easy to be with. Kate was nothing like you."

"Kate?" Gen's radar went on immediately. She hoped she hadn't just walked into another situation like the one she'd had with Keaton.

"Kate's another teacher at school. We went out a few times before I met you."

Gen didn't need to be a cop to know that there was more to the story than he was sharing. "Why are we nothing alike?"

"Kate…just wasn't who I thought she was." Squeezing her hand, he said, "I'm so glad you and I can just be together and have a good time."

After pulling into her driveway, Cary smiled. "We'll have to do this again sometime."

"I'd like that."

Together they walked up the small flight of stairs to her apartment, taking care to dodge the pots of geraniums Bonnie had just planted. Gen's mind was working overtime. If only Cary knew how confused she felt. She'd never been comfortable dating. Now, after making the terrible assumption that her friendship with Keaton had been more romantic than it was, she wasn't too comfortable with herself, either.

It felt strange to realize Cary may see her in a different light than Keaton ever had. "I'd better go in. I'm due in early tomorrow." Why was she finding this so difficult?

"Okay." He surprised her by holding out his hand.

She took it. Only Cary Hudson could make a simple handshake seem so much more than just two hands briefly touching.

His hand was warm and solid and masculine, his fingers gentle against her own.

And then, well, things weren't so sweet any longer. Cary tugged Gen toward him and clasped her other hand. Now they stood mere inches apart.

That's when he kissed her. A hundred feelings rocked forth—surprise, panic, pleasure and the amazing knowledge that the very calm, cool and collected Cary Hudson really knew how to kiss.

Gen held on tight and hoped he wouldn't step back anytime soon.

Because when he did, Gen knew she would miss kissing him, being in his arms. She would miss…him.

GEN STOPPED BY THE high school the next afternoon. After looking a bit more into the damage done to Melissa Hudson's car, she'd decided the girl had been nothing more than the victim of a random prank. Dean hadn't sounded too surprised when she'd called him at his office in downtown Cincinnati.

However, she decided the news was as good a reason as any to see Cary in person.

After all, hadn't Sergeant Conrad encouraged her to be more visible in the community?

After registering in the LEHS front office, she walked down the school halls. Gen nodded to a few kids, then paused as she saw a girl who looked awfully familiar. After a moment, Gen placed her. It was Amy Blythe—Melissa's neighbor. Gen had done some checking on the girl, mainly because there wasn't anyone else to investigate.

What she'd found had broken Gen's heart. Like Melissa, Amy was an only child who lived with her dad. But that's where the similarities ended. While Melissa had blossomed from both her father's and uncle's attention, Amy had veered in the other direction and retreated into herself when her father hadn't been able to recover from the loss of his wife, after her death in a car accident.

When Gen caught the girl staring at her, she approached. "Any idea how to get to the math department? I keep getting turned around."

"Sure. Math's in the north wing. In the

basement. Go down a flight of stairs, then turn left."

The school really was a maze. "Mind reminding me where the stairs are?"

Amy looked around, her blond curls bobbing. "Go past five—" She stopped. "Never mind. I'll take you."

"It's no trouble?"

"No…I needed to go there, anyway."

"Thanks. I really appreciate it. I'm Officer Slate, by the way."

"Amy Blythe."

"Nice to meet you."

Amy looked surprised but said nothing. Within minutes they came to the stairs then started descending, the metal gently clanging under Gen's thick-soled shoes and Amy's boots.

Even though she already knew the answer, Gen asked, "What grade are you in?"

"Junior."

"Ah. You're almost done with school, then."

"Yeah."

There it was. A curious mixture of relief and worry. Gen knew the feeling. Back in Beckley, she'd been both eager and scared to leave high school and find out what the world held in store for her.

They turned left, their footsteps echoing on the worn linoleum. Gen noticed the halls were narrower in the basement, the ceiling slightly lower. Small windows and canister lighting lit the way.

The space felt claustrophobic.

Once again she was glad to be a cop. She'd hate being stuck down here day after day. How Cary did it, she wasn't sure.

Gen decided to make one last-ditch attempt to make a connection with Amy; the girl looked as if she could use a friend.

"I'm new here in Lane's End," Gen said, sounding even to her own ears like a Chatty Cathy.

"I'm not. I can't wait to leave."

This wasn't going to be easy. "I felt that way about my town. I grew up in a place smaller than this, in West Virginia."

Amy wrinkled her nose. "I would have wanted to leave there, too."

Gen laughed. They turned the corner and stopped short when they spied Cary and a pretty woman with silvery-blue eyes in the hall.

"Ah. There's who I was looking for. Do you know Mr. Hudson?"

"Sure. Everyone does."

"Who's he talking to?"

"Ms. Daniels." Amy frowned at the lady, so slim and graceful in a straight skirt and heels. "She teaches Spanish."

Hearing the definite coolness in Amy's voice, Gen prodded a little. "Not one for foreign languages?"

"Not one for *her*. She and Mr. Hudson used to date." Amy scowled. "She broke up with him. I wonder why he's being so nice to her now?"

So that was Kate.

Gen couldn't hear what they were saying, but she had to agree with Amy. Cary and Kate looked as though they were getting along just fine.

Gen felt a stab of jealousy. What was the big deal? Cary and Kate were likely just discussing school matters. "Well, I'd better go interrupt so I can get on out of here," Gen said, pushing herself away from the wall. "Thanks for your help."

But to her surprise, Amy had already left.

CARY LOOKED HAPPY to see her. "Hey, Officer."

"Hi." Gen grinned at him, then turned her attention to the other woman.

"This is Kate."

Since Kate's warm smile had vanished, Gen played it cool. "Nice to meet you." Turning to Cary, she said, "Can you spare me a minute? I've got a couple of items to go over with you."

"Sure. I'll see you, Kate."

"Bye, Cary. Officer."

As they entered Cary's room, Gen was struck again about how much she enjoyed being in his presence—being surrounded by all things Cary. Even a place as innocuous as a math lab reminded her of the things she liked about him. Never mind that she found him especially attractive in his work garb. The faded, well-ironed khakis, button-down shirt with the frayed collar and cuffs and serviceable loafers made him seem both extremely handsome and terribly approachable.

"I just wanted to tell you that after speaking to a few more people, I don't think we're going to find the person who damaged Melissa's car. Vandalism is extremely tough to prove since it's difficult to find eyewitnesses."

Cary leaned against his desk. "I thought as much." He looked at her again, his brown eyes patiently waiting as though he had all the time in the world.

Now she was out of things to talk about. A true professional would back away and leave.

She stepped a little closer. "Sorry I don't have better news."

"Don't be. You tried your best."

"I stopped by here because Dean had sent word he was going out of town. And I wanted to…let Melissa know what was going on." She winced as she heard her jumbled explanation. Why did he make her so flustered?

"Yep. Dean's gone for the night." Cary looked at her carefully, his hands stuffed in his pockets. "So. What do you think of my home away from home?"

"Your classroom's nice, but I'd hate being stuck in the basement," she said honestly.

He laughed. "So would everyone else.

All of us in the math department wonder what we did to deserve this."

He was so open with his emotions. Open and assured. She was coming to realize that with Cary Hudson, what you saw was what you got.

Obviously she had a tough time being so honest. It was in her nature to be guarded and question everything. Which was why, even though she wanted to just stand around and visit, she couldn't do it without a reason. "Well, then…"

Teachers walked by his room, their voices floating in. Cary looked at the doorway and smiled. "Everyone's talking basketball."

"With good reason. That game was great."

His eyes lit up. "It was terrific."

When he didn't mention going to the next one, Gen felt embarrassed. What if their kiss hadn't meant much to him?

What if he wasn't really over Kate?

"Well, then…I best get going." She turned to walk away.

To her surprise, he clasped her wrist. "Gen…when am I going to see you again?"

She didn't know what to say. "I don't

know." Ugh. She sounded like a juvenile kid who'd just been on her very first date.

But he didn't laugh at all. Instead a small smile played on his lips. "I'm going running tonight with Sludge. Why don't you meet us?"

"Do you mind if Sadie tags along?"

"Not at all. Behind the Corner Café is a trail. I usually jog it a couple of times a month. Will you join me?"

She wanted to. And running with beagles sounded relatively innocent.

"I'll be there. Six?"

"Six's good. I'll see you and Sadie there."

THAT AFTERNOON AFTER her shift, Gen called herself ten times a fool. She needed to stop mooning over Cary. She was making too much of their date and of their kiss last night. She was too excited to see him in a few hours.

This girlie giddiness was so completely unlike her. Obviously it was time to think about something else.

Making a sudden decision, she high-tailed it downtown to Natalie's Nursery and went on in.

An attractive elderly lady with a short pixie cut and hazel eyes greeted her. "May I help you?"

"I hope so. I want to take up gardening." Gen glanced at the lady's name tag. "Veronica."

"Anything in particular?"

"Yep. I want to grow Easter lilies."

"That's excellent for this time of year!" she said brightly. "We've got some beautiful lilies. Come along now."

Gen followed the lady down three aisles of various plants until they stopped in front of a collection of grubby little plants, each about four inches tall.

"Here we go."

"They don't look like much."

Veronica laughed. "They will. That's the amazing thing about flowers. Give them love, attention, water, light and they'll turn into things of beauty."

With determination, Gen plopped four of the sad little shoots into her cart. "Tell me what I need to do."

Like the seasoned professional she was, Veronica loaded her up with gardening gloves, fertilizer, beautiful clay pots for each plant, potting soil and the prettiest little copper watering can Gen had ever laid eyes on. The total came to eighty-seven dollars.

Eighty-seven dollars for a hobby she wasn't even sure would stick! Gen now knew it was official. She was an excellent cop...but when it came to hobbies, she was clueless.

CHAPTER EIGHT

CARY WASN'T SURPRISED to see Gen arrive for their run on time, Sadie neatly confined to the back of her car by one of those pet gates he saw in stores. He had a feeling Gen was always punctual and organized.

As he and Sludge watched her hop out and attach a leash to her dog, he was pleased to see her bare legs under a pair of teal nylon runner's shorts. Finely muscled and toned, they were nothing short of fantastic.

Genevieve Slate didn't just jog every so often to stay in shape. She was about to run him into the ground.

"Hi," she said, walking Sadie over. Within seconds both beagles circled each other, sniffing and getting acquainted. Cary was relieved to see that Sludge didn't look hostile in the slightest; instead his tail wagged happily.

"Hi." Pointing to Gen's well-defined quads, he said, "I'm guessing you run more than I thought."

"Some." Her cheeks colored slightly. "I've been known to be competitive when it comes to training," she said casually. "Give me a goal and I'll achieve it."

"What about your dog? Can she keep up?" Good grief, what was he doing—trying to play one-upmanship with a beagle?

"Usually." Gen's chin rose a little. "What about Sludge?"

"He can hold his own."

"Let me stretch and then we'll be off." Without a trace of self-consciousness, she grabbed a foot and bent her leg behind her, stretching her thigh, then did the same with her other leg. After that, she leaned forward to touch her toes. Cary did his best to do the same, though his gaze kept straying.

She really was pretty.

To get his mind off those legs, he pointed to the hill behind them. "This is where the trail starts. Does that look okay to you?"

"Yep."

"Great, then." With an excited howl from Sludge, Cary took the lead and led them up the trail. That was the last time he felt in control.

Gen and Sadie had clearly made this run before. Nimbly the two of them tromped along the hard-packed dirt, zigzagging along the path like seasoned soldiers on a mission.

He and Sludge were used to a slightly slower pace. Okay, a lot slower. Still, they kept up, but he couldn't resist a few jabs. "Do you always run like this?"

She glanced at him over her shoulder. "Like how?"

"Full-out."

She smiled. "Pretty much."

Cary narrowed his eyes. Sadie looked worn out; her head drooped and she kept looking at soft patches of grass with longing. And, if he wasn't mistaken, Gen was panting, too.

As sweat trickled down his back, he charged forward, Sludge grunting with the effort. Thankfully, it didn't take too long to pass her. "There's a nice stopping point a few yards from here. You want to take a break?"

"I'm fine."

"You sure? Sadie looks tired." He was dying!

Sadie popped her head up when she heard her name, but Gen shook her head. "No, we're fine."

Within minutes they approached a pair of iron benches. Cary had glanced at one with desperation when Sludge howled and pulled away.

Taken aback, Cary tripped on a root. As he tried to right himself, Sludge yanked again. This time Cary's hand relaxed as he tried to keep from falling…but it was too late.

Sludge found freedom. Nose to the ground, the fur along his spine popped up and his tail jutted out. With a victory howl, he was off in search of rabbits.

"I'll get him," Gen called out, she and Sadie running to Sludge. But things didn't go too well for her, either. She slid on a patch of damp leaves and she reached out instinctively to a nearby tree trunk to re-gain her balance.

It was all the invitation her dog needed. In an amazing burst of energy, Sadie ripped free of Gen's grasp and darted through a thicket of trees, diving under a bush just as a brown rabbit hopped into view.

Gen whistled. "Sadie. Here, girl."

Sadie looked at Gen, then turned back to Sludge's retreating tail and the rabbit. Nature won out. Sadie shook her head, slipping her loose collar over her head and to the ground.

As the beagles disappeared into the woods, Gen groaned. "I can't believe she just got out of her collar. She's never done that before."

"Sludge has escaped, but not for a while." Cary shook his head as he walked over to stand beside Gen. "Don't worry, though. I don't know about Sadie, but Sludge is basically lazy. He'll come back in a minute after he chases that rabbit."

Gen nodded. "I hope you're right. The last thing I want to do tonight is hunt for our dogs."

Two happy barks echoed in the distance. "I don't think you'll have to. They haven't gone too far yet," Cary said. "Let's give them a minute and ourselves a break."

Wiping sweat from her brow, Gen nodded and sat down on the soft grass. "Until the dogs went wild, this was fun."

Cary sat down next to her. "It was. You're some kind of runner, Slate."

"You're not so bad yourself." Gen paused for a moment before leaning against him. "I was having a hard time keeping up."

"Keeping up?" He laughed. "You were running like a mountain goat."

"Thanks for the comparison."

"Anytime." She felt so good against him, he wrapped an arm around her shoulders. Gen curved in a little closer, bringing a moment of peace. This was what he'd always wanted. A woman with no pretenses, a woman who was easy to be with.

Despite her skittishness, he found Gen refreshing. He liked how she tried to get along with other people and make friends. He liked how she chose to live in an upstairs apartment over Bonnie instead of taking one of the new condos on the outside of town. He liked how she ran fullout, never imagining that his pride might take a beating.

With Kate, he'd always felt that there were two different Kates—one who was by his side, the other just watching, judging. With some surprise, he realized that Kate Daniels had worn him out.

After a few moments of content silence, Gen inched away. "I guess we'd better start a search and rescue," she said regretfully as she stood up. "It's going to be dark pretty soon."

"Hold on," Cary said, reaching into a zippered pouch in his jacket. Triumphantly he pulled out a handful of dog biscuits. "Sludge! Sadie! Treats!" he called out.

Gen started laughing as a howl, followed by the sound of rustling bushes, broke the silence. In no time, the two beagles raced forward. Cary handed them each two treats.

Gen took the opportunity to slip Sadie's collar back on and to grab the end of Sludge's dangling leash. "I'm glad you were prepared."

"Me, too," Cary agreed. Holding out his hand, he said, "Let's try a slower pace. What do you think?"

A small smile lit her eyes as she placed her hand in his. "I think that's a fine idea," she murmured as they headed back toward their vehicles.

As he rubbed a thumb over her knuckles, he wondered if she was as happy at that moment as he was.

"I DON'T REMEMBER THE last time one of us was asked to rot in hell," Cary said as he stared at the black letters spray painted across the wall outside Kate's classroom.

Evan frowned. "When Mitch called me at five this morning to tell me that someone had broken into the gym and left...*this,* I asked him to repeat it—slowly. I was completely shocked to find out that we'd been vandalized. I haven't seen grafitti in this school in a couple of years."

Cary nodded. "The last incident I can recall is when a kid threw a couple of bricks through the library window."

They moved aside as Dave, Christy and a few other teachers joined the crowd.

Without taking his eyes from the scrawled letters, Evan said, "Anybody else get a note on their walls?"

"Not that I've heard," Monique, one of the science teachers, said.

Brushing her hair back, Christy whistled low. "'I hope you rot in hell.' That has teenage angst written all over it."

Evan grimaced. "This seems personal. I think we'd better have a staff meeting."

After glancing at his watch, he said, "Immediately. I don't want the rumor mill going crazy before we have a chance to figure out what's really going on." Turning to Christy, he said, "Would you mind rounding up the others? I'm going to make a quick call to the police station."

"No problem."

"I imagine the police are going to want to pull both teachers and students for questioning," Evan added, looking at the scrawled words on the wall. "I'll see if Mitch can cover this up with something in the meantime. It'll keep the fingerprints to a minimum and help tone down some of the excitement. See you in ten."

Turning to Kate, Cary noticed the fine lines around her mouth. "You okay?" he asked after the group disbanded.

"Honestly? I'm not sure."

"I bet it's just a prank."

Kate frowned at the writing. "I don't

know about that. I'm more inclined to agree with Evan on this one. Those scrawled words feel personal."

Though he'd been almost out of earshot, Dave turned around. "Kate, I wouldn't stress about it. You know how kids are—they push buttons."

Cary was impressed. Dave had been his greatest defender when Kate had left him. For Dave to try to make Kate feel better, Cary figured he was shaken up. "Dave's right," he said. "I've only heard good things about you from the kids."

Kate shook her head. "Obviously somebody doesn't feel that good."

As THE STAFF congregated in the large, modern-looking library, several teachers patted Kate on the shoulder or sent appraising looks in Cary's direction. With some dismay, Cary realized more than one person had noticed him comforting her.

The general murmuring and chatting came to a complete stop when Evan entered, his expression grim. "The bell's about to ring, so I'll be quick. Here's the deal, gang. We've had an incident of vandalism, near Kate's room. I expect the police to be here shortly. Please give them your total cooperation if they ask you any questions."

A voice called out, "When did this happen? How could a kid get into the school so early?"

"As far as I know, somebody broke a window near the gymnasium and slid in through the opening sometime this morning," Evan replied. "Mitch found the writing when he arrived at five." He looked at Kate. "We got the okay to paper the walls. Mitch's doing that right now."

"Thanks."

Evan nodded, his expression sympathetic. "Gang, if the kids ask what happened or what was written, tell them nothing. The less said, the better."

Kate raised her hand. "Should I trade classrooms or something? If the police are wandering around, it's going to be tough to hold my students' attention."

"Let's keep everything the same until we get more direction from…" He looked at his notes. "Officer Slate."

Dave raised an eyebrow at Cary's sharp

intake of breath. Looking from his friend to Kate to the empty hall behind Evan, he dared to grin. "Tough day, Hudson," he said as the bell rang.

GEN HAD NO REASON to be agitated, but she was. She and Sam had been asked to go investigate the graffiti—Sam mainly there as backup since the lieutenant had informed her that this was to be her case.

And the case looked to be a pretty involved one.

They weren't spreading the word, but some in the station were predicting that the slashed tires and the graffiti would turn out to be connected. Gen's instincts told her that was right on. She'd seen plenty of graffiti and blown tires in her line of work, but not slashed tires and hate messages. Especially not in a small Mayberrylike town such as Lane's End. For two incidents of vandalism to happen so close together, it was worth at least examining the possibility that the same person was responsible.

Gen was just considering how to question the school's administration when Sam joined her.

"We found some fingerprints and took samples, but I doubt they'll amount to much," Sam said. "This prank was probably done by a student, so there's little we can do to prove they were here last night instead of during the normal schoolday."

"Did you take pictures of the graffiti?"

"Yep. Samples of the paint, too."

"I'm still waiting to speak to Principal Miller." Glancing at her notes, she said, "I think we should go ahead and give approval for the custodian to paint over the writing. Do you have a problem with that?"

"No. I feel the same way, Gen."

His support felt good. She'd just smiled when the principal's door opened.

"Officer Slate? Sorry to keep you waiting."

Gen stood up. "No problem. Sam, you want to join us?"

"No, that's okay. I'm going to deliver the evidence to the lab. See you back at the station."

After a quick nod of acknowledgment toward Sam, she held out her hand. "I'm Gen Slate."

"Evan Miller. Nice to meet you. Come on in."

As Gen stepped into his office, she couldn't hide her surprise.

Evan chuckled. "I get that a lot," he said, motioning to the colorful array of framed artwork done by kids. The room was bright and vibrant, leaving no doubt in anyone's mind that Principal Miller cared about children. "I never was one to need diplomas and such decorating my walls." Seating himself behind a desk, he said, "Want a cup of coffee? I don't function too well unless I've ingested a full pot."

Gen felt herself warming to him immediately. His gray hair and easygoing attitude complemented his teddy-bear-like build. She was also a fan of anyone who liked coffee as much as she did. "I'd love a cup. I suffer from the same problem."

While they waited for his receptionist to bring them two cups, Evan said, "I hear you're new to Lane's End."

"I am. I was with Cincinnati PD for a while and in West Virginia before that."

He grinned. "I thought I heard a hint of a Southern twang calling."

A young woman brought in two mugs of coffee. After thanking her, Evan sipped thoughtfully. "When Mitchell, our custodian, arrived this morning, he discovered the message near Kate Daniels's classroom and contacted me. I called the staff together, then rang the police."

Gen wrote down Mitchell's name. "I take it the graffiti isn't a usual occurrence?"

"No. That's not to say this high school doesn't have its share of problem behaviors. We certainly do. But spraying a hate note on a wall is out of the ordinary."

"Tell me about Kate Daniels," Gen asked, feeling vaguely uncomfortable. In some ways she thought Kate was her rival for Cary, which was completely ridiculous.

"Kate is an excellent teacher."

"How about as a friend to kids? Does she get along well with everyone?"

"Kate's not the kind of teacher kids talk about. She's fair. Knows her stuff. Strict." He shrugged. "That's why this is a bit of a puzzle to me. I've never heard the kids speak strongly about her one way or the other."

Gen tried another angle. "And in the community, among staff members?"

Evan's blue eyes clouded. "She's a single woman. I'd say she has a habit of dating men who might be a little influential to her career—school board members, et cetera—but I'm assuming it was a student who did this."

Feeling a little self-conscious, Gen said, "I heard Ms. Daniels was once involved with Cary Hudson. Since his niece's tires were slashed recently, I'd be remiss if I didn't ask if you thought there was a connection."

"Cary. Hmm. That's an interesting idea."

"Why is that?" She already knew a lot about the man, and everything she'd seen she'd liked a lot.

"If I had to guess who'd be the target of a prank like this, Cary would be just about the last person I'd name. He's an extremely popular teacher."

Gen had seen that for herself during the two basketball games they'd attended. "Why do you think that is?"

"He cares about everyone. People respond to that."

Gen shifted uncomfortably. She for one had definitely responded to him. The way he smiled, the way he'd curved an arm around her when they'd waited for their beagles. The way he'd held her so close when they'd kissed.

Focus!

"I'd like to speak with Ms. Daniels."

"We figured as much." After glancing at the clock, Evan said, "First bell will ring in ten minutes. Can you wait a moment? Kate has the next two periods off."

"No problem."

"You can sit in the conference room at the end of the hall, if you like. I'll tell Kate to meet you there when she's free."

"If you don't mind, I'd rather wander around and go to her classroom." She checked her notes. "She's in Room 212?"

He nodded.

After getting a generous refill of coffee and a quick set of directions, Gen left the office and walked in the general area of the foreign language department. Though classes were in session, she saw several teachers and students wandering around. Most spared her a quick glance.

Gen spotted Melissa at her locker. Gen hesitated for a moment, well aware that the girl would probably not be pleased to see her after the questioning about the tires. But, to her surprise, the blonde called out a greeting. "Hi, Officer Slate. How are you?"

"Fine. You?"

Melissa blew at her bangs. "Stressed. I have two tests today and pictures for the paper this afternoon. When I washed my uniform, I think I forgot to pack my bow."

"Ah."

With a grin, Melissa turned to her. "I know to you a bow might not seem like much, but when I'm the only girl with my hair messed up in the photo, believe me, it's not good."

"Good luck finding it. And with the tests, of course."

"Thanks. Why are you here?"

Gen wasn't sure how much the student body knew about the graffiti. "Just a little business." She stepped back. "Have a good day."

"You, too."

As Gen walked on, a few doors opened and students, some taller than her, filtered out. Again most gave her a wide berth. She saw Melissa's boyfriend, Brian, with two other basketball players. All were wearing letter jackets and stood a full head taller than everyone else.

Finally Gen passed a sign announcing the entrance to the foreign-language department. After double-checking the room number in her notebook, she turned the corner.

She saw the hastily covered-up wall, the paper tamped securely down on all sides to prevent curious onlookers. The janitor probably wouldn't risk removing the paper to paint until the students left the area.

She was just about to take a quick glance at the damage herself when a bell rang and kids exited Kate's classroom. After the steady stream cleared, Gen poked her head in.

Kate was sitting at her desk, with her head in her hands. Instead of wearing a crisp suit this time, Kate wore slacks and a slightly rumpled lime-green twinset.

Gen cleared her throat.

Kate popped her head up.

"Sorry. I didn't mean to startle you."

"Don't be." Lines of worry eased as Kate attempted a smile. "Come on in, Officer Slate. Evan warned that you'd be stopping by."

"I'll try not to take up much of your time."

"Don't worry about it. If you can help, I'd appreciate it." A shaky hand betrayed her nerves. "This graffiti thing has done a number on me."

"Any idea who could have done it?"

"No. My classes are pretty cut-and-dried. Foreign language is a requirement. I try to do the best I can, but most of the kids are in my class because they think Spanish might be easier than French or German or Latin."

"Or have visions of Cancun on spring break," Gen said with a smile.

Kate laughed. "That wouldn't surprise me."

Feeling slightly uncomfortable because of what she knew about Kate and Cary, Gen said, "Melissa Hudson's tires were slashed a few days ago. I'm wondering if there might be a connection between the two."

Genuine surprise filled Kate's gaze. "I don't see how. I don't teach Melissa."

Knowing she had to ask the question, Gen took a deep breath. "But you did date her uncle."

Surprise, then concern, entered Kate's eyes. "Yes. But it wasn't serious."

"I see."

Leaning forward, Kate said quickly, "Did Cary tell you it was serious?"

Gen held up a hand. "Listen, I'm just trying to figure some things out." After several more questions, she walked toward the door. "I'll let you know when we get a lead."

"Thanks," Kate said, slumping back in her seat.

Following her map, Gen made her way back to the stairs, then followed them down and around the corner until she reached the math department.

Second period was still in session for another few minutes, so she leaned against the wall and thought about Cary and Kate together.

Gen couldn't deny they would've made a cute couple. Both were tall and slim, both had the type of polished good looks she'd never cultivated. But still…Gen didn't think they were a good fit.

Maybe it was just the day's events that had her feeling suspicious, but Kate seemed too brittle for Cary.

He needed someone who wouldn't care if his dog got her messy or worry if she'd forgotten to put on makeup or was addicted to burgers and donuts.

From her spot in the hallway, Gen could hear his voice as he joked with the kids. She chuckled when he gave one of them a hard time about wearing shorts and sandals in the cold spring weather.

After the bell rang and the kids exited, Gen waited a good two minutes, then stuck her head in.

His eyes crinkled in greeting when he saw her. "Genevieve Slate. We ought to stop meeting like this."

Gen bit her lip. On the contrary. To her way of thinking, she couldn't see him often enough.

CHAPTER NINE

OH, CARY LOOKED good. He was clad in khakis again, but this time wore a black knit long-sleeved shirt that accentuated his athletic build. Her strong attraction made her uneasy, which in turn made her speak without thinking. "So I may have been wrong about this being random vandalism."

Cary cocked his head, managing to look her over and chastise her all at the same time. "I'm fine, thanks. Good to see you again, too."

She ducked her head. She had come across like a bulldog with a piece of raw meat…all tenacity and no charm. How was it she could hold her own in a job that required her to deal with difficult situations all the time, yet she acted like an immature schoolgirl around men?

Hoping to smooth things over, she said,

"When I told you that I have a hard time combining work and my personal life, I wasn't kidding."

"And here I thought I was part of both."

"You are."

"Glad to hear that," he said with a smile.

Oh! Now how did a girl respond to that?

Cary had a gift for easy conversation and for making her completely aware of her attraction to him. Recalling that her assertive personality had gotten her nowhere with Keaton, she found herself fumbling over words. She also had the uncomfortable realization that she was blushing again.

It was mortifying. Honestly, how could Cary look so calm and collected when she felt an attraction that bordered on all-consuming?

As if he'd read her mind, his gaze softened. "I'm sorry. I don't mean to be a pain in the neck. To answer your question, I don't see why Kate's spray-painted wall would have anything to do with Melissa."

They both started when Mitch interrupted. "Hey, Cary. Tell the students in your next class to go up the other staircase, would ya?" He glanced at Gen. "Your buddies said they're all done getting finger-prints, so I'm going to go ahead and paint if that's okay?"

"Sure thing, Mitch. Thanks."

Quickly Gen asked a few more questions about Kate's students and Kate's history at the school before closing her notebook. "I'd better get going. My sergeant's going to want a report."

"Oh, right. I'll be seeing you, Gen."

She stepped away, feeling it almost diffi-cult to do, as if she was disengaging herself from a magnetic pull. "I'll call you when I find out anything."

"You do that. I'll look forward to hear-ing from you...about anything."

His smile, combined with the honest comment, made her step closer. Forget-ting about her inability to have a normal conversation and the fact that she was sup-posed to be working, not flirting, she met his gaze. "Um, how's Sludge?"

"He's missing Sadie." Glancing at her lips, he said, "We ought to go running again. Soon."

"If you want—"

"I do," he interrupted just as a group of

kids walked in. "Name the day and time and I'll be there."

Gen scurried out before his class became completely aware that Lane's End's newest cop had a thing for their teacher.

HOURS LATER, CARY took another deep breath before exhaling quickly, ready for the last mile of the six-mile trek. Beside him, Sludge was running at a brisk pace, looking for all the world like a Mighty Dog advertisement.

It was amazing that a beagle with such an unhealthy appetite could run so well.

The day was cool but sunny. The welcoming rays fell down upon Cary's shoulders as the biting temperatures stung his face, making him feel energized. After the first mile, his shoulders had relaxed.

The day had been a nightmare. After Gen's visit, rumors about the graffiti and what was going on between him and Gen had started flying. All day teachers, kids and parents had talked about nothing else. To top it off, Kate had stopped by his classroom before she'd left, looking so vulnerable that he'd hugged her. That little bit of affection had been witnessed by more than a couple of people, including Christy, who'd glared at him for being such an idiot.

Cary couldn't blame Christy. Hadn't he moped around for weeks after his and Kate's breakup, wondering how he could have misjudged her so completely?

Kate's visit had been followed by one with an emotional Melissa, who hadn't been able to find some missing bow. Cary had counted the minutes until he could finally escape the high school and find some freedom running on the bike path.

Gen's claim that the graffiti and Melissa's tires were related had been jarring, but not as much as the realization that although he found Gen incredibly attractive, he had no idea if she felt the same way about him. Gen seemed to wear a coat over her emotions and thoughts, she kept so much to herself. He'd watched her walk out of his classroom feeling as mixed up and confused as any of the teenagers with him.

Sludge's howl stopped both his feet and his meandering thoughts. Gripping the dog's leash a little tighter, he looked to the right, where Sludge's attention was securely focused.

"Good thing you have that dog with you," Dean called out as he approached. "I've been trying to get your attention for five minutes."

Cary pulled the headphones from his ears and turned off his iPod. "Sorry. What's up?"

Dean shook his head. "What isn't?" He pointed to his worn jeans and old leather tennis shoes. "Mind walking for a little while?"

"No problem." Sludge happily led the way, wagging his tail at everyone they passed and sticking his nose into every available bush and shrub. As for himself, Cary eyed his older brother carefully. While it wasn't unusual for Dean to take a walk on the trail, leaving his downtown Cincinnati office before six o'clock was.

"Melissa told me about the graffiti at the school," Dean said. "Why didn't you call me about it?"

"I was going to tell you about it later."

"It was outside of Kate's classroom, right?"

"Yep."

"Did you get a chance to talk with Kate?"

Cary did not want to go there. "I did. Everything's fine."

Dean eyed him closely before shaking his head. "Okay." After a moment, he spoke again. "You know, our relationship doesn't have to stay the way it's been."

"What are you talking about?"

Dean shrugged. "You helped me get through my divorce. I depend on you to help me with Melissa. You handled most of the details when Mom and Dad died. But it can work the other way, you know. I could, for once, be there for you."

But that wasn't Cary's way. He liked being needed, not being the one in need. "Thanks, but really—I'm fine."

"Gotcha." Dean matched his pace for a few yards, remaining silent, but not for long. "What's Evan going to do about the vandalism?"

"He called the police. Gen Slate—the officer who spoke to Melissa about her tires—stopped by and talked to me."

"Oh, really?" A speculative gleam entered Dean's eyes. Had Melissa told her dad about Cary's date? "What did she say?"

Cary had definitely liked running better with just Sludge. "She thinks the damage to Melissa's tires and the graffiti might be related."

Dean's steps faltered. "How sure is she?"

"I can't answer that. Gen didn't say much of anything."

"Hey, didn't you take Gen to the game the other night?"

Cary almost laughed at Dean's not-so-subtle question. "I did. We went out running, too," Cary said, recalling how warm and sweet she'd been in his arms when they'd kissed good-night.

Dean chuckled. "Ah."

"What?"

"Now I get it. You like her."

"Maybe." Cary winced as he heard his words. He sounded so juvenile.

"You're sounding like the kids you teach."

Cary grunted at his brother's ability to read him. "What do you want me to say?"

"Something along the lines of…'I like this woman. I want to date her.'"

"Oh, please. You're one to talk. Who've you been out with lately?"

"Susan Edwards. Last month."

"Oh, yeah. Now I remember." They'd both known Susan forever—she, too, had lived in Lane's End all her life. After years of not-so-subtle hints, Dean had finally asked her out and had gone on one date with her.

"You can keep your heckling to a minimum, thank you."

"Not my fault Susan talks a mile a minute."

Dean rolled his eyes. "That's putting it mildly. But at least I went out."

"Good point."

They walked some more, talking about the NCAA tournament that was about to claim the rest of the country's attention. "I think Melissa really loves Brian," Dean said.

Cary knew where he was heading. "I think you're right."

Dean swallowed hard. "Melissa's just a girl."

"She's growing up."

"You don't think…? What I mean is—I

have a feeling maybe her relationship with Brian is more serious than I'd thought."

Though Cary had always thought of himself as pretty much Melissa's second father, this was one of those times where he was really glad he was only the uncle. "You probably should have one of those father-daughter bonding talks soon."

The expression on Dean's face would've made Cary laugh if he wasn't so glad he wasn't in his brother's position. "You're good with kids. Maybe—"

"Nope. Not even for a minute do I want to talk to her about boys. I did my part when she was little—I cooked her grilled-cheese sandwiches and played tea party."

"I wish Mom was around."

"Me, too. Mom would know what to say."

"Did Dad say much to you?"

Cary chuckled. "Nope. Our conversation didn't last longer than ten minutes." Recalling how their normally unflappable dad had stuttered during the chat about girls, Cary said, "I guess it's never easy."

"No, I guess not."

When Sludge started panting heavily,

they turned and headed back toward the parking lot. "You know, Melissa's a smart girl. I'm sure you'll figure it out."

Dean grinned. "I'll do my best." Deftly switching topics, he said, "Hey, since there's no game this weekend, some guys from work are going out for pizza. Want to join us?"

"Thanks, but I'll pass. I've got tests to grade and a couple of other things to do for work." Cary didn't dare mention that he was hoping Gen would call.

"Suit yourself. So…you sure you're okay?"

"Yeah. I'm fine."

The look Dean gave him said loud and clear that they both knew he was lying. Gen Slate had affected him in a way no woman ever had before.

WHEN EVAN CALLED AT six in the morning, Cary knew the news wasn't going to be good. "What's up?"

"We had a smoke bomb in one of the lockers. It was Melissa's, Cary."

The news hit him hard. A week had passed since Kate's wall had been spray painted, enough time to make him think that they'd all overreacted to the vandalism.

"When?"

"Early this morning. I called the police and spoke with Sergeant Conrad." After a brief hesitation, he said, "It might be best if Melissa stayed home today—most of her stuff was ruined. Maybe you could stay with her."

Knowing Dean was going out of town again today, Cary thought keeping Melissa company was a good idea. But he also thought Evan was being a little too cautious. "Any other reason besides keeping an eye on Melissa?"

"There have been three incidents in two weeks. Each one has a connection to either you or Melissa. It's a little too coincidental."

"I have a job to do, Evan. I can't stay home forever."

"I know, but twenty-four hours isn't going to do any harm and it will give the police time to look into the situation and maybe find the guilty party."

Cary glanced at his kitchen table, which was littered with his teacher's guide and lesson plans. "What do you want me to do about today? My plans are here with me."

"Hold on." In the background Cary could hear the principal speak briefly with a few people. "We're sending an officer over to get your things. She's going to leave for your house in a couple of minutes."

She? Cary had a very good idea who that was going to be.

GEN'S PULSE BEAT rapidly as she knocked on Cary's door. Only she would be excited to see Cary for such a bad reason.

Every time she was around Cary, her nerves stood on end. The last time they'd talked, she'd had her professional cap on way too tight. During the past week, she'd considered calling him but had been reluctant, worried that maybe she had misread his offer. Now work responsibilities made her feel edgy once again.

Things would be so much easier if she wasn't investigating anything at his school.

Gen held her breath as she heard Sludge bark, and Cary opened the door.

"Hi, again," she said, hoping her voice sounded friendly and not terse.

"Hey. How'd you luck out and get errand duty?"

She laughed, relieved things were okay between them. "Two words—*new officer*."

"Come on in." He looked uncertain. "Do you have time?"

"I do. Actually, I've been asked to speak with you about a few things."

Cary led her into his front room, where they'd spoken with Melissa. "The chairs were my parents'," he said, indicating the two wing chairs by the window. His chatter revealed that maybe he wasn't so cool and collected, either. "They're worn but comfortable."

She sat down on the denim one and had to agree. Not that she was eager to relax.

After a moment, Cary brought her a stack of books and papers, as well as a folder with a set of typed notes inside. She placed them next to her own notebook. "Thanks."

He leaned forward, resting his elbows on his thighs. "Gen, tell me about Melissa's locker."

His eyes were so velvety-brown, his gaze

so full of questions and concern, that she took a little fortifying breath.

Briefly Gen gave Cary the details about what they'd found, including a cut-up staff photo of Cary, which shocked him. "I think it's now pretty clear someone is desperate for your attention. Cary, we need a list of students who you think might be capable of something like this."

"I know a lot of kids, but I can't think of any who would actively want to hurt Melissa."

"What about you? Have you had trouble with a student lately? Know of anyone who could be holding a grudge?"

"Not really."

Gen wrote down some notes, doing her best to act calm and collected. But inside her stomach was churning. It had been hard entertaining thoughts about Keaton when he'd been her partner, but this was twice as hard.

Instead of concentrating on Cary's answers, she was remembering how good it had felt to be with him after their run. How much she'd enjoyed kissing him.

But all that mattered now was her job.

She was a professional—and finding out who was so angry at Melissa and Cary had to come first. Later on, if things were as good as she hoped they were between her and Cary, she could concentrate on that. Closing her notebook, she stood. "I'll get your things to school."

He reached out and gripped her hand. "Whoa, there. That's it?"

His fingers were warm, his gaze completely leveled on her. "What…what do you mean?"

"I mean, you've told me nothing."

"As of right now, there's nothing to tell, Cary," she said softly.

He didn't release her hand. Instead he tugged her a bit closer. "What's going to happen next?"

For a split second she thought he was talking about them. But he couldn't be… right? Clearing her throat, she murmured, "I'm going back to your school to deliver your things and then report to Sergeant Conrad."

"Gen…how've you been?"

Snap. Just like that, all thoughts of the

case slipped away. Slowly she exhaled. "Truth?"

"Of course."

"I…I'm all scattered inside."

"I feel the same way." He inched closer, ran a hand along her arm, the touch marking her through the thin fabric of her shirt. "Yeah?"

"Uh-huh." Oh, he smelled so good! She stepped closer. Cary pulled her into a hug. "Maybe later you can stop by," he whispered. "Have a soda. Eat some nachos. You know…when you're off duty."

Nachos brought back thoughts of Mexican food, which brought back thoughts of the kiss after their date. Her mouth went dry.

"After we eat, I'll rub your shoulders." He leaned back to look at her. "You're looking awfully tense, Slate."

She was feeling pretty tense all of a sudden. "I really better get your things delivered. I mean, think of all those poor math students dying to do equations."

He laughed. "I can promise you, not one of them is going to care about not having anything to do. At the moment, I'm not thinking too much about algebra, either."

She was having a hard time concentrating on anything herself. "What are you thinking about?"

"Us. You." He tilted his head. "I've been thinking about you a lot."

This was where she should admit the same thing. Looking into his eyes, she knew he was waiting for her to give him some kind of sign. Something to propel him forward, to stop dancing around their attraction and to step into a real relationship. But…she wasn't quite ready.

What if she was wrong? She couldn't bear the hurt she'd felt when Keaton had rejected her. Hastily she stepped back and picked up his books from the table. Holding them to her chest, she said, "I really better go deliver these. I'm on the clock, you know."

"I understand."

Did he? She didn't. At the moment, nothing made sense. "We should talk later."

"I agree. But first we should do this."

He leaned forward to kiss her. Oh, she wanted it, but if he kissed her that minute, she was going to be even more mixed up. And late.

She really needed to get going. "Cary…maybe…I don't think so."

"I definitely do." Cary reached out and cupped her chin, ran those long fingers along her jaw. "I can't stay away from you. I don't want to, anyway."

No one had ever talked to her like this. So honest, so unafraid to meet any situation full-force. Her hands went limp, causing the books to slide to the floor.

One landed on her boot. She hardly noticed. "Later, when we talk, we should discuss this attraction between us," she said.

He brushed his lips along her jaw. "Uh-huh?"

"Yes. We can come up with a plan."

"A plan?" he asked, kissing her again.

Work was definitely overrated. Finally giving in, Gen slipped her hands around his neck and kissed him back.

He tasted minty and warm and exactly the way she remembered. Like everything she'd dreamed a kiss could be when she'd stayed home on Saturday nights in Beckley.

Then she remembered what she was supposed to be doing. Breaking off the kiss, she pulled out of his arms. "I really gotta go. Now." Hurriedly she picked up her notebook, gathered his books and ran out.

"I'll call you, Gen," he said as she rushed to her cruiser.

"Great," she called out, tossing his poor, beaten-up textbooks onto the passenger seat before slipping the car into Reverse and pulling out of his driveway.

She couldn't resist looking for him out her rearview mirror as she drove away. He was leaning against his garage door, Sludge by his side, watching her go.

It was almost enough to make her believe in love.

GEN PLAYED PHONE tag the rest of the day with Cary. Her first message stated she had nothing to report. Her second said she'd see him later.

While she was in a meeting, she received a call from him. "I know we talked about getting together tonight, but I can't," he'd said, his voice regretful. "This vandalism thing's affected Melissa more than I thought. As much as I want to see you, Melissa needs me tonight. Call me tomorrow."

She phoned him hours later. "I didn't want to go to bed without telling you good night." With a deep breath, she added, "Thanks for calling. I'll talk to you tomorrow."

CHAPTER TEN

THAT NIGHT, BONNIE knocked twice on Gen's door before letting herself in and speaking her mind.

"Your dog is a menace," Bonnie stated matter-of-factly as she stepped into Gen's apartment with a container of homemade chili and enough brownies to make the most ardent chocoholic happy. "She needs a warning label pasted to her side."

Saying Sadie was a menace was pretty much like saying she was a beagle—they were one and the same. After gesturing for Bonnie to take a seat on the couch, Gen said, "What's she done this time?"

"Nothing good. First of all, she howled nonstop all day."

That certainly didn't sound menacing. "Hmm. I wonder what was bothering her."

"I wonder what wasn't." With a steely-eyed glare at Sadie, Bonnie continued.

"Around lunchtime I took pity on your girl and let her out. The minute that dog was free of the house, though, she strode right over and trampled my petunias I just planted."

"The petunias, huh?"

"Oh, don't give me that policewoman look, Officer Slate," Bonnie said crisply. "Sadie zeroed in on the only blooming thing in the whole backyard. Before I could get to her, she'd already begun her search-and-destroy mission."

That sounded premeditated. "I don't know. I just don't think she's that smart."

"Humph. She's got you fooled."

Gen bit her lip, knowing it would be futile to argue. Sadie learned from her poor behaviors. If Bonnie kept taking her out when she howled, Sadie would continue to howl. Loud and often.

Of course, terrorizing the petunias was a mystery.

Because Bonnie was still giving Gen a look that would do any interrogator proud, Gen went through the motions of acting as if she understood why Sadie was the way she was. "Have you seen any rabbits around? Sadie loves to chase rabbits."

"Not a one." If daggers could have gone shooting out of her landlady's eyes, Gen would need a hundred stitches.

O-kay. "I'll try to figure out why she's howling so much and will replace your petunias. Thank you for—"

"Hold on there. I haven't even gotten to the worst part."

"I'm afraid to ask."

"Sadie ate my chicken pie."

Gen glanced again at the chili she was holding. "Huh?"

"I made a pie for some people at church. After the howling and petunia incidents, I brought Sadie in to clean her paws, and that's when it happened."

Gen joined Bonnie on the couch. She distinctly recalled sharing with Bonnie the cardinal rules about living in harmony with Sadie. Rule number one: never leave her alone in the kitchen. Rule number two: never forget rule number one.

Bonnie just kept talking. "I wasn't gone more than three minutes when I heard my favorite pie plate clatter to the floor and break in two. That rotten beagle didn't even have the decency to slow down or slink away when I came back in and gave her a piece of my mind. No, ma'am. She just started eating faster!" Finally Bonnie paused to take a breath.

Gen glanced at Sadie. Contrary to Bonnie's description, the beagle did now look genuinely contrite. At the moment, she was attempting to fit her pudgy girth under one of the kitchen chairs. It wasn't going too well.

"I'm sorry about the pie and your plate." Looking at the bright white Tupperware container, Gen said, "Where did the chili come from?"

"I made it as soon as I cleaned up that mess."

"Oh, my. You must have been in the kitchen all day."

"I was."

"I'm so sorry, Bonnie. I'd have never asked you to take her out today if I'd known she was going to be so much trouble."

"Don't you fret. It's Sadie I'm put out with, not you."

Warily Gen examined Sadie. Now safe

under the table, she was staring at Gen with her familiar soft brown eyes, looking for all the world like a candidate for the Westminster Dog Show. "I think she feels really bad now."

Bonnie looked skeptical. "She's probably just digesting."

Gen searched for anything to talk about besides her dog's poor manners. "I saw Cary Hudson again today."

"Did you two go out on another date?" Bonnie asked hopefully.

"No." Not wanting to reveal too much, Gen said vaguely, "There's been some vandalism going on at the high school, as you may have heard, and I had to speak to him."

"Yes, word's been going around town that things are a real mess and Cary's smack-dab in the middle of it."

Gen hid her grin. One of the drawbacks of living in a small town is that secrets don't stay secret for long. "I've never asked, but do you know Cary very well?"

"Fairly well," Bonnie said, her petite frame reminding Gen of Alice in Wonderland. Curling her feet underneath her, she added, "I go to the same church as the

Hudsons. Have forever." Looking at Gen fondly, she said, "Oh, you should have seen Dean and Cary when they were small."

She wished she had. "Cute?"

"As all get-out! But hardworking, too. Cary and Dean were typical pastor's children. If anyone ever needed a helping hand, they were put into service. They helped mulch the neighbors' beds, raked leaves. They participated in church services, sang in the choir. It almost became a kind of joke guessing what Pastor Hudson might have Cary and Dean do next."

"It sounds nice," Gen said, imagining what a younger Cary would have been like.

"They were nice. A happy family." With a frown, Bonnie shook her head sadly. "It was a sorrowful day when those boys lost their mother to cancer, then their father right after. Pastor Hudson was a wonderful leader, and their mother a giving woman."

Taking the opportunity to pick Bonnie's brain, Gen said, "I'm having a hard time figuring out why Cary or Melissa would be targets of vandalism. Based on what you've been saying, both seem so popular."

"I'm sorry, Gen, but I have no idea

who could be responsible. Luckily that's your job and not mine." Gesturing toward Gen's tiny back porch, Bonnie hopped up. "What's all this?"

With a groan, Gen realized all her brand-spanking-new gardening supplies were sitting in a pile out in the open, her plants looking anemic. "Oh. Easter lilies. I'm going to take up gardening."

"Best take it up soon or you're going to kill these little guys." Bonnie scurried to the sink, grabbed a glass off the counter and filled it with water. "You might not have heard, but you're supposed to *water* plants," she said, handing Gen the glass.

Obediently Gen poured a small amount into each pot. "I didn't know you could be so sarcastic."

"I'm finding out new things about you, too." Gesturing toward the plants, she said, "I'll help you plant them tomorrow, if you like."

"Thanks."

"Well, it's six-thirty—time for you to eat and for me to go deliver chili to Mrs. Johnson. She hurt her leg last week."

"Do you need some help?" Gen asked, thinking that Bonnie wasn't too spry herself.

"Not yet. You go eat now, dear."

After Bonnie's departure, Gen gratefully heated up the bowl in the microwave, added cheese, then sat down with a cold drink and the television for company.

Sadie, never one to let a hot dish be ignored, circled her affectionately, as if Gen were some kind of fool.

Balancing her bowl of chili on her lap, Gen reached down and scratched Sadie's ears. "I'm not falling for that trick. I know exactly how your mind works."

Sadie dipped her head down in disgust, finally lying right on top of Gen's feet. "That's okay, girl. I'm ready to relax, too."

As sitcoms flashed before her, Gen thought of Bonnie and her chicken pie. Of the bowl of chili and Mrs. Johnson. Like cogs in a wheel, they all seemed to go together... Bonnie helping everyone as she saw fit...Mrs. Johnson, like Gen, delighted to eat a home-cooked meal.

Which made her think of home. Next thing she knew, Gen was calling Margaret for the second time in two weeks.

"'Lo?" Meg said the moment she picked up the phone. "This had better be good, because I've got a four-year-old having a temper tantrum."

Laughter erupted before she could stop herself. "Hey, Margaret. It's Gen. What happened to your fancy caller ID?"

"I'm on an extension. Wait a sec and let me calm Emily down." Pure pleasure tinged her voice when she returned. "I can't wait to hear why you're callin' now."

Gen ate another bite of chili as she heard Margaret fuss with Emily. Within seconds the soothing sounds of Barney the dinosaur filtered through the phone.

"Emily does love Barney," Margaret said by way of explanation. "Is everything okay? Anything wrong?"

"Everything's fine."

"You sure?"

"I'm fine. I'm home. Eating chili with Sadie."

"Oh, chili sounds good. I'm eating a pea-nut-butter-and-jelly sandwich with Emily while the baby's sleeping."

Because Margaret's voice was still tinged with expectation, Gen said, "I didn't

really call for a reason…I was just thinking about you."

"How's the gardening coming along?"

"Not so good. I've bought the plants but
haven't had time to get them in their pots."

"It's a start. Even though you don't ever
have to call for a reason, I'm thinking you
did. Let me guess—a certain man is still
on your mind."

"You'd be right."

"So…are you actually dating?"

"I'm not sure." So far she'd gone out
with Cary twice and had shared a couple
of pretty incredible kisses, but she couldn't
say if this was going to be a regular thing.

"What's the guy's name?"

"Cary. He's a schoolteacher. He has a
beagle, too."

"So you've got lots to talk about."

"Sometimes." Gen didn't have the heart
to admit that so far most of their conversations had been about vandalism.

"I bet things are going to work out just
fine. Just don't be afraid to be yourself."

That was good advice. Gen only wished
she could learn to follow it. "Margaret…do
you ever wish we were closer?"

After a pause, she replied, "Always."

"I guess I've pulled away."

"I'd say you have, some. But I let you do it, which isn't good, either. I'm ashamed that I let you do it. It was easier than to judge my life against yours."

"What? You're perfect."

"Hardly. You're the one with the exciting job. I'm only a stay-at-home mom."

"And Momma loves you for it. Everyone loves you for it!"

"People might admire me, but they brag about you."

Gen was genuinely stunned. "I never imagined that."

"'Course you wouldn't—Momma was never one to give compliments freely. You know how that goes. On my wedding day she told me it was really too bad I had a pimple on my chin."

Gen laughed so hard the chili almost fell into Sadie's waiting mouth. "You looked gorgeous. Everyone thought so."

"Everyone but you-know-who." In the background, Gen heard the door slam. Gen could hear Shane calling for Margaret in between the sobs of their little boy.

"Uh-oh. I'd better go. Call me back later. Hey…maybe one day I could come out and see you."

"I'd like that," Gen said, surprised with how much she meant it.

"Good. Ask me and I'll do it. Talk to you soon."

By now the chili was cold, but that didn't matter. What had just happened with her sister made everything seem okay.

CHAPTER ELEVEN

CARY ARRIVED FIVE minutes early for the scheduled meeting in the conference room, but it turned out he wasn't the only person eager to get things under way.

He was the last to arrive. "Hi, everyone."

Lieutenant Nate Banks shook Cary's hand. "Good to see you again, Cary."

Also in the room were Evan and Gen. Though she was eating a blueberry muffin and sipping a large mug of coffee, she looked more serious than usual. "Hey, Cary," she said.

"Gen," he murmured as he sat down to the left of her.

Since Evan was speaking on the phone in a low voice, Cary used the time to reflect on the past few days. February had faded into March, and with it, three more days had passed since the last incident of vandalism. The graffiti had been painted over, the smoke bomb forgotten. The Lions had won their final game in the district play-offs and were now heading toward the regional championships with one of the best records in the area's history.

Cary's contract was in and the indecision forgotten. He'd gotten in two more six-mile runs, and Sludge hadn't terrorized anyone besides the UPS guy in two days.

His gaze strayed to Gen, who was still concentrating on her muffin. Although he hadn't expected her to launch herself into his arms, something a little more warm and personal would have been welcome.

What had happened? The last time they'd kissed, Cary had been sure there was something special between them, a connection. Even more significant had been their open, honest conversation.

But ever since, things had been sketchy. After Tuesday night had been canceled, Gen had been busy on Wednesday. He'd had a late meeting Thursday night, that had been out. And now here they were, face-to-face, uneasy again.

Lt. Banks cleared his throat. "After much

discussion, we decided to place an officer at Lane's End High for the next few weeks."

"Yes. It would have a myriad of benefits," Evan stated.

Cary winced. Their principal only used words like *myriad* when he was uncomfortable.

Continuing, Evan said, "Not only do we have the recent cases of vandalism, but things are bound to get rowdy if our team keeps winning."

"Never say *if,* Evan," Cary joked, attempting to lighten the atmosphere. "The Lions are going to go all the way."

Evan held up crossed fingers. "I just don't want to jinx it."

Gen and the others laughed. After a few more minutes, the lieutenant closed his notebook. "So it's all set. Gen, until further notice, you'll be assigned to Lane's End High. Finish whatever you need to do at the station, then return here as soon as possible."

After glancing in Cary's direction, Gen nodded. "All right, if you're sure this is where I need to be."

"This has been your case from the start,

Gen. It's a good fit. I'll go over your duties in more detail at the station. For right now, I'd like you to get a feel for the place."

Gen stood up as Lieutenant Banks paused at the door before leaving. "Thanks, Nate." When she sat back down, Cary noticed Gen looked a little stunned. Was she disappointed with the assignment?

Evan handed her a packet. "I took the liberty of outlining your day and highlighted areas where your expertise would help."

"Thanks." She took the paper without a word. Cary noticed she hardly looked at it.

Evan either didn't notice or didn't care, because he kept talking. "As you can see, it would be beneficial if you patrolled the halls, entryway and parking lots and talked to some of the kids to get more information. Maybe you could join some of Pat Brown's health classes, steer a few discussions toward subjects the students might have questions about, such as drinking and driving. Students might feel less uncomfortable that an officer's around if they got to know you."

"That sounds fine."

"Now, as far as possible suspects, I wrote down Cary's and Melissa's schedules. Thought you might want to pay special attention to who they come in contact with."

"I'll do that."

"If you turn the page over, you'll notice there's a ball game Thursday night. We'll want you there. Crowd control is going to be an issue."

Cary shook his head. Evan must have wanted to be a cop in an earlier life. He sounded almost giddy about the thought of helping plan a police officer's day…and helping in the capture of the kids who were messing up his school.

Finally Evan left for his next meeting, leaving Cary and Gen alone.

"I wish things could have worked out for us this week," he said, not even pretending to care about anything but their relationship.

Surprise…and a hint of longing entered her eyes. "I do, too." Tossing the papers on the table, she looked at him directly. "Especially since things between us are going to be a little strained."

"What are you talking about?"

"Working at the school and being around you so much is going to be tough for me," she murmured. "When I'm on duty, I take my job very seriously. I hope you won't mind."

"I wouldn't have it any other way," Cary said, thinking that her tenaciousness was what made her so special to him.

She flipped through Evan's notes before glancing at him again, looking all business. "Is there anything in particular you'd like me to do while I'm here?"

There was that wall again. High, thick and most likely made of concrete. There was no way he wanted it to stay there. "Kiss me in dark corners?"

"Besides that."

Because he could have sworn she was blushing, he took pity on her. "There's nothing I can think of that you need to do, Gen."

Her blue eyes blinked as her cheeks definitely flushed. "I'm sorry—my mind's going in a hundred directions right now. This assignment took me completely off guard. May I stop by your classroom at the end of the day?"

"If that's what you want."

Standing, she looked at him again, her expression soft. "I do want that. I'll see you later," she said in a rush before striding out the door.

"COFFEE BREAK, SLATE?" Sgt. Conrad asked later that afternoon as he moseyed over to the coffee machine.

She held up a bag of chips and a Coke.

"Just having some lunch while reading up on my next assignment."

"I heard you're still on the high school vandalism case. Better be careful or you might get asked to the prom."

Gen chuckled. "I might even be tempted to say yes, since I wasn't asked the first time around."

Conrad raised an eyebrow. "Rumor has it you were less than thrilled by the assignment. Want to tell me why?"

Could she take a risk and let her guard down with the sergeant? "It—it wasn't the job, sir. It's a personal matter."

"Ah. You and Cary Hudson."

Did everyone within a hundred-mile radius know her business? Since there was no point in denying it, Gen nodded.

Sgt. Conrad leaned back. "Cary's a good guy. My little brother went to high school with him."

She should have known. "Do you think we seem like a strange couple?"

"Not at all. My wife would call you both 'good people.'"

She knew exactly what that meant. Back in West Virginia, the term was a true compliment. "Good people" were ones you became friends with, respected, introduced to your mother. "Thanks."

"Let me know if you need a hand with the case, Slate. You don't have to work all on your own."

Conrad's offer felt genuine, not condescending.

It also felt a little like a life preserver, just standing nearby, waiting. It was comforting. "Thank you."

"WE'RE GOING TO enjoy working with you, Officer Slate," Evan said at the staff meeting that afternoon. "Please let us know if we can help you in any way while you're here."

"Thank you. I'm looking forward to getting to know all of you and the students." She turned to Evan. "I think your suggestion of joining the students' health classes is a great idea. If the kids have a reason for my being here, they'll be more likely not to see me as a threat. If I just wander the halls, rumors will start flying."

A woman in the back motioned with her hand before beginning to talk. "I have a feeling more kids are going to know you than you might imagine. Especially since you're obviously a good friend of Cary's."

The comment drew more than a few jokes and jabs from the group.

Though it had been said without rancor, it grated Gen's nerves. Now she was going to have to investigate the vandalism and fend off unnecessary conjectures about her relationship with Cary Hudson at the same time.

Gen looked at Cary. He was chatting with two other teachers, not paying any attention to her in the slightest.

Then, realizing the majority of the people

were still waiting for a coherent response, Gen shrugged. "I hope before I leave I'll be able to count many of you as friends. I'm new to Lane's End, as you know."

Her neatly sidestepped remark caused several other people to chuckle. Finally Evan called the meeting. "See everyone tomorrow."

Gen gathered her materials, thinking to herself that she shouldn't be so sensitive about everyone's interest in her personal life. She'd known living in a small town created such situations.

The appearance of the health teacher saved her from further introspection.

"I've got some ideas for our class, if you have time to see them," Pat Brown said.

"I'd love to see your materials."

As Pat led the way to her classroom, Gen looked around with interest. Just like students—and cops—the teachers and staff members were standing around talking. Others were in their classrooms, either erasing or writing on whiteboards.

After two right turns, they came to Pat's large room. Filled with bright yellow bulletin boards, it was energetic and inviting.

With little fanfare, Pat picked up a packet from the corner of her desk and handed it to Gen. "Here's the information I mentioned during the meeting. There are some lessons about drinking and driving, consequences for speeding, signs of drug use, that sort of thing."

Gen nodded. "I have pamphlets I can bring in, too."

"Great. Maybe we can start each class with a brief introduction, then open it up to questions. That should help you get to know the students quickly."

They spoke for a few minutes more before Pat looked at the clock. "I'd better get going. I take water aerobics at the community center a couple of nights a week."

Gen noticed Pat looked healthy and toned. "That sounds fun."

"I'm sure you, being a cop and all, could probably run circles around what we do, but if you ever want to join us, let me know. We're always happy to see a new face in class."

The offer seemed genuine, and Gen was touched. "Thanks."

"You're welcome." Pat grabbed her coat.

"One more thing—don't let all that teasing about you and Cary get you down. Nobody means anything by it."

"I'll try not to," Gen said but knew that would be a hard promise to keep. Her feelings for Cary were so fresh, the last thing she wanted to do was have their relationship be fodder for the town.

It was now almost five; her meeting with Pat had taken longer than she'd anticipated. With a sigh, she hurried to Cary's room, hoping he hadn't already left, not wanting him to think that she was blowing him off once again.

Lane's End High had been through so many renovations and additions the floor plan reminded Gen of a maze for laboratory animals. Honestly, she needed a breadcrumb trail to find her way to Cary's room. She'd just backtracked and was staring at the library when Cary approached.

"Let's see. You either need a good book or you're completely lost."

"I'm so glad to see you. I've been wandering in circles!"

"I'm glad I found you then," he said with a smile.

"Me, too. I'm going to need an escort to help me through the halls on Monday."

"I won't be able to help you Monday, but I can be of service right now." He held out a hand, which she took gratefully.

He looked her over. "So…I guess you've made peace with the assignment?"

Embarrassment welled, making her cheeks heat. "Yes."

They walked down the next hall, turned a corner and suddenly came upon the exit to the parking lot. As they walked outside, the sun greeted them. "It's almost five and still sunny as ever."

"I'm glad. I hate it when the days are so much shorter in the winter."

"Are you free tonight?"

"I am. Until I hear differently, I'm on school hours." That was one part of her new assignment she wouldn't find fault with. "I'm looking forward to it—I haven't had a regular schedule in years."

"So maybe you'd like to grab some pizza?"

Nothing sounded better. "I'd love some pizza."

"Good." His steps slowed. "Oh, no."

"What's wrong?" She followed his gaze. Spray painted in the same bright red that was used on the wall outside Kate Daniels's classroom was the word *NO* scrawled across the side of Gen's cruiser.

Looking around, Gen scoped the area, but it seemed completely empty. Pulling out her cell phone, she quickly punched in the precinct's number. "Hey, Amanda. I need Sergeant Conrad or Lieutenant Banks, please." When Sgt. Conrad got on the line, she said, "I'm in the high school parking lot. There's been another incident of vandalism."

"What happened?"

"My car. Someone had a field day with a can of spray paint."

"I'll be right there, Gen. Secure the area."

"Yes, sir."

After she clicked off, she apologetically turned to Cary. "I'm afraid I can't make it for pizza after all. I, uh, will call you later, okay?"

To her surprise, Cary shook his head. "Oh, Gen, you're crazy. Do you really think I'd just leave you here? I'll stay with you as long as you want."

Relief slid through her at his words. Though she knew she could handle the situation, it was nice to know she wouldn't have to do it alone. "Thanks."

He kissed her brow. "Anytime, Slate. Anytime at all."

CHAPTER TWELVE

Pictures had been taken, followed by fingerprints. After questioning the few staff members who had still been on campus at the time, Gen made plans to ask the remaining teachers if they'd seen anything suspicious. Finally, Sergeant Conrad asked two other officers to take Gen's squad car back to the station.

Through it all, Gen was torn between duty and her desire just to react. She felt angry and violated. Now she knew what it felt like to be a victim and she didn't care for the feeling one bit.

"Well, that's it for now," Sergeant Conrad said. "Slate, you're going to be busy tomorrow."

"Yep. If you'll give me a lift to the station, I'll file this report—"

"Whoa. You're off duty, Slate."

"But—"

"I saw your time card. You reported in at six this morning." He glanced at his watch. "I think twelve hours is long enough. Sam's going to type up the notes."

"But my car—" When she'd picked up the cruiser at the start of her shift, she'd left her Outback at the station.

"Sam and another officer are going to drop it off at your home later," Cary said, gently curving an arm around her shoulders. "Everything's taken care of."

"You sure?"

Her sergeant's eyes softened. "Positive. Go take a break, Gen. See you, Cary."

"Bye, John," Cary said as he unlocked his Explorer's doors. "Let's order a pizza, Gen."

After seeing that Conrad and Sam definitely had everything under control, Gen finally relaxed. "You know, pizza sounds even better to me now. I just realized I'm starving."

"Me, too."

"So…your place or mine?"

He grinned. "How about we go to yours? If we go to mine, I have a feeling we'll run into Melissa and Dean. They're going to ask a dozen questions, and I'm just not up for that right now."

"Me, neither."

As Cary drove out of the parking lot, Gen couldn't deny that she was shaken up, not only because she'd been personally touched by the vandal, but she now knew the perpetrator was targeting people who had a connection with Cary.

As if reading her mind, Cary murmured, "This has something to do with me, doesn't it?"

"I think so."

"Any idea why?"

"Not yet." She leaned her head back against her seat. "As far as I know, you're well-liked in the community, so the only thing I can think of is that someone might have a crush on you." Attempting to lighten the mood, she added, "Besides me."

Her words hung between them like clothes on a line. Yet again, she'd blurted her inner thoughts. She waited for him to contradict her, to patiently explain how she'd completely misread his feelings, but the exact opposite happened.

"You've got a crush?" he asked, looking pleased.

"Yeah, I do." She studied his profile, liking the way a hint of a beard was visible on his face. Liking the way he never shied away from his feelings or from hearing hers.

He was a far different man than Keaton was. Though Cary, too, had seen his fair share of heartache—losing both his parents, having to give up some of his own needs to help his brother and niece—the experience didn't seem to scar him. He still acted hopeful about the future, was content with himself.

At that moment, Gen wanted to grab on to him and hold on tight.

It felt good to be with him. She was incredibly thankful he'd stayed by her side this evening. Maybe, despite her fear of being hurt again, they did have a chance together. Maybe—

A horn blared to her left.

Cary grinned when she jumped. "Settle down, Slate. It's not a crisis—it's the horns from the band. Look at them!"

Sure enough, twenty kids wearing jeans,

old tennis shoes and black T-shirts were lined up in front of the community center, playing the Lane's End High School fight song. The mascot, a large golden lion, held a tub of candy and was passing it out to children who came forward.

Pinned across the center's front porch was a pair of sheets with the words *Go, Lane's End!* painted in bold black letters.

Cary laughed as cars all around them honked their approval. "The more things change in Lane's End, the more they stay the same, huh? You and I aren't the strangers we once were, yet we're still here in the same place, doing the same things."

Gen couldn't agree more. While she'd been attempting to uncover a vandal and get a handle on her relationship with Cary, life had gone on. Once again, she was stuck in LEHS traffic.

"I've been so focused on what's been going on with you I completely forgot about the tournament," she admitted with some surprise.

Squeezing her hand, he teased, "I wouldn't mention that to another person around here."

"I wouldn't think of it."

"Because you've had such a long day, I'm going to do you a favor when we get to your place."

"Rub my back?" She hadn't been able to forget about his earlier promise.

"I will. Then I might even put on the game and teach you everything I know about basketball."

She rolled her eyes. "Just because I forgot about the tournament doesn't mean I don't enjoy the game. I know the basics."

"Xavier University's playing at seven. You up for it?"

"Maybe. Can we have mushrooms on the pizza?"

"Only if you have something to down it with."

"I have Coke."

"Then it's a yes."

Gen chuckled to herself as he pulled in to her driveway. There was something very good happening between them. A tension, an awareness she sensed had never been between her and Keaton.

And more importantly…how had she not realized something so vital in creating a strong relationship had been missing in her feelings for Keaton?

"I HAVE TO ADMIRE A gal who can almost single-handedly finish a whole pizza."

"There was a reason I ordered two."

Cary raised his second Coke to her in a toast. "Here's to planning ahead."

Gen playfully clicked her can with his before taking a sip.

As the Xavier game ran into the third quarter, he was happy to see that they were up by ten. They'd been looking good tonight. Good enough that he thought he could pull his attention away for a few minutes.

"So...did you do any hunting and fishing while growing up?"

"Yep." She tilted her head and studied him carefully. "You ever fly-fish?"

"Nope."

Gen leaned back. "One day I'll take you to the New River. There's some real pretty sections where the fishin's good. I'll outfit you in waders and we'll have a go of it."

Cary laughed. "Your West Virginia voice is talking."

Unexpectedly she blushed. "I guess it was. I try to tame the twang, but when I think of things I used to do when I lived in Beckley, I can't help but think of them in terms of the language I used growing up."

"You shouldn't try to get rid of your accent. It suits who you are."

Gen's eyes widened. "Isn't that funny? Do you always think of yourself as an algebra teacher?"

"I certainly hope not!" Sipping his drink, he studied her. "But I see what you mean. Some vocations are like that."

She leaned closer. "So what would you say you are?"

He shrugged. "Too many things…and in some ways, not anything. I'm Dean's brother. We're closer than most. I'm Melissa's uncle. I wouldn't have missed living next to her for anything."

Thinking back to how he'd wanted a change just a few short days ago, he shook his head. Now he couldn't imagine living anywhere else. "Lately I've been hoping for more."

"Like what you had with Kate?"

Cary sighed. "Looking back on the time

Kate and I were dating, I've realized we weren't really 'together.' Now I can see that we both knew it…I just didn't want to face the truth."

Finding out about Cary's past was interesting. "So before Kate, did you ever have a serious girlfriend? Even in college?"

"Not in college. I dated Sarah Williams during my junior and senior years in high school."

"Pretty name."

"Yeah," he said fondly. "Wow, I haven't thought of Sarah in years." Turning to Gen, he smiled at the memory. "Sarah not only went to my school, she went to my church. I was with her constantly."

"Pretty?"

"Oh, yeah. But in a way, her looks didn't matter, you know? After a while, she was just Sarah."

"What happened?"

"The usual. She went away to college and we grew apart." He shook his head. "I worry about Melissa sometimes. She and Brian are so close and he's heading to college next year. I don't know what she's going to do or what I want her to do. If she and Brian break up, she's going to be devastated. If they stay together, she's going to spend her whole senior year wishing she was someplace else."

Belatedly realizing he'd just droned on about more than she'd asked him, he said, "What about you?"

"Me? Well, hmm. No, I never did the serious-boyfriend thing."

"Not even in high school? I would have thought the boys would love a girlfriend who liked the things they did."

Gen shook her head. "If they did, they didn't tell me about it. In a lot of ways, I stayed in the shadows. My sister, Margaret, was homecoming queen and prom queen and student council vice president. She's petite and feminine and caught the eye of every boy in the county. I was just her sister."

The hurt in Gen's eyes stung Cary. Imagining how awkward that must have felt and knowing how easily a guy could chase after a pretty, popular girl, he said, "Was that hard for you?"

"Back then, it didn't bother me too much. Meg's social success made me even more determined to move away from Beckley and do something different. I started looking at colleges my sophomore year of high school."

"Did you always know you wanted to become a cop?"

"Pretty much. I wanted a job where I could be outside a lot, not chained to a desk. I thought about being a firefighter, but frankly, I wasn't sure if I could pass the physical tests. I was a lot leaner back then."

"So then…"

"I earned an associate's degree, then applied to the Cincinnati PD. The rest is history."

"Except why you're here."

"I needed a change." Closing her eyes briefly, she said, "I had thought—mistakenly—that I had finally found the guy I would spend the rest of my life with. Ultimately it turned out he didn't feel the same way as he fell in love with someone else. I thought I could handle working with him after that, but I was wrong. It was then I decided it was time to move on."

Her eyes wide, she reached out to grip

Cary's arm. "I've never told anyone about him. About Keaton."

"I guess it was time then." Wrapping an arm around her, he held her close.

As though she was embarrassed about her admission, she turned to the TV. "Hey! Xavier's up by twelve."

It was too bad he couldn't have cared less. At the moment, Gen was the only thing on his mind. The way her long, sleek black hair felt like liquid silver whenever it brushed against his hands. The way her dark-blue eyes could look sad and hopeful at the same time. The way every inch of her was finely toned and incredibly strong yet seemed so delicate, daring him to touch her soft skin. Giving in to impulse, he traced her collarbone.

"I've been thinking about doing that for a while."

Her lips curved up, her expression tentative. "Do you still want to rub my back?"

"I thought you'd never ask," he murmured.

Without another word, Gen presented her back to him.

Annoyed with himself for feeling like a

schoolboy, he began kneading her muscles. He felt a knot above her shoulder blade and massaged it.

Gen moaned. "Oh, that feels good."

Yes. Yes, it did. Gen's skin was velvety-soft and lightly tanned. The fresh scent of lemons surrounded her. He breathed in deeply and sighed, wanting to kiss her again.

He dug deep for a little control. "Okay. This is what we're going to do. You're going to watch the game, and I am going to rub your back."

Gen raised an eyebrow as she looked at him over one shoulder. "I thought that's what we were doing?"

Almost against his will, he spanned her waist, caressed her lower back.

Gen rolled her spine forward.

As Xavier rebounded and the crowd on the television went wild, Cary tried to resist the urge to pull her back into his arms and kiss her senseless.

CHAPTER THIRTEEN

FROM THE MOMENT the first bell chimed, Gen felt way too out of place at Lane's End High.

Rather than befriend her or volunteer any information, students avoided her like the plague. They talked in whispers and darted the other way when they saw her coming.

Her inability to blend in was extremely irritating. Sgt. Conrad would rip her to shreds if she didn't make this work. What she needed was to lose her natural reticence and be warmer and chattier. If the run of vandalism didn't end soon, eventually a person was going to get hurt, and everyone affiliated with the case would feel the sting of lost opportunity.

When the first health class of the day started, Pat Brown introduced her. Gen strode to the front of the room with more than a little trepidation. She'd never had to address a bunch of kids before, and any hiccup could affect the students' opinion of her.

"Hi, everyone. I'm Officer Slate and I'll be on campus for the next month."

Not one of the thirty kids looked as if they cared.

Gen pretended they did. "I'll be acting as a liaison between you and the police department. Schools in Cincinnati have police officers on campus on a regular basis. We're testing it out here."

One boy slumped in his chair in the back raised his hand. "Aren't you really here because of the smoke bomb and the graffiti?"

"Well…yes. That's the other reason."

The class seemed to breathe a collective sigh as they realized she was going to speak straight, tell it like it was.

"*My* job is to keep everyone safe so you can do *your* job and get an education. I'm hoping we can be partners. Someone around here has made it his or her business to make the environment here uncomfortable. These pranks may seem harmless, but they can get dangerous, and someone might get hurt."

Gen paused to let her words sink in. "If you know anything about what's been happening, or who might be involved, you need to speak to me or a teacher. I think we'd all feel horrible if someone got hurt and it could have been prevented."

"Listen to what Officer Slate has to say," Mrs. Brown said. "She's here to make sure we all stay safe."

Only silence met that suggestion.

Gen was just wondering what else she could talk about when a hand rose. "What do you think about the Lions?"

"I think they're great," she said in relief. "They might even have a chance to get to state."

A gal in the front row smirked. "A chance?"

Obviously those were fighting words. Since anything was better than stone-cold silence, Gen egged the students on. "Given the team's past record, I'd say 'chance' is a little generous."

As expected, the room erupted into shouts and laughter.

Mrs. Brown chuckled from her post near the back of the room before she called out, "If you wanted to get them talking, you couldn't have picked a better topic, Officer Slate."

"Call me Gen," she said with a grin.

"YOU ALMOST LOOK like a freshman," a woman commented to Gen as she patrolled the halls two hours later. "You've got that same scared look they all do."

Gen smiled. "I'm not scared, I just keep getting lost in this building."

"Where are you headed?"

"Lunch."

The gal's face brightened. "I'm heading there, too. You buying or did you bring your lunch?"

Gen held up her brown paper bag.

"Smart woman." As they left the math wing and walked up a flight of stairs, the other woman introduced herself. "I'm Christy Pardue, by the way. We met the other day. I teach with Cary."

Recognition clicked in. "Now I remember. You had your hair up and glasses on before, right?"

"Yep. Good memory."

Gen nodded in acknowledgment. "Thanks for helping me through this maze."

"No problem. How's your day going?"

"It's going."

"Have you done this before? Been assigned to a school?"

"Not in a long time and not by myself." Feeling as if she should be more positive, she added, "It's a nice change of pace, though. Far better than directing traffic in the rain."

"Especially if you catch whoever's been causing so much trouble. The batch of pranks has got us all on high alert. Things like this just don't happen around here. At least I didn't think so."

"In my experience, unexpected things happen everywhere. They just make more of an impact in a small town. But I'm confident we'll find out who's behind all this. Spray painting my cruiser was so blatant I think he or she wants to get caught."

To Gen's surprise, Christy looked at her for a long moment. "Maybe he or she does," she murmured before making another turn. Christy then stopped and opened the door to a large staff room.

"We wondered if you were ever going to take a break," an older man in wire-rimmed glasses said as she and Christy claimed two chairs. "How's your first day going?"

Christy gave everyone a knowing look. "Right now, Officer Slate is attempting to negotiate the labyrinth we call Lane's End High."

"Good luck," another teacher called out. "Took me two weeks to find the copy room."

"I can believe it," Gen said with a laugh. "I took two wrong turns and ended up in the wrestling room."

As others introduced themselves, Christy put change in a pop machine and pulled out a Coke. Gen did the same.

After they sat down, the older guy spoke again. "So have you run into Matthew Reid yet?"

"I'm not sure."

"You'd know him if you saw him. He's currently wearing a skull-shaped nose ring."

"It sets off his bald head," another teacher said.

"No, I haven't seen him," Gen replied. "What's he like?"

"Smart as a whip. Sarcastic. You're going to love him."

"I'll be on the lookout for him, if I get the chance. Maybe he'll stand out in health class."

Christy nodded as she opened up a carton of yogurt. "Evan was smart to place you in Pat Brown's room. She's a good teacher and she's got a nice rapport with most everyone."

Two more teachers entered the room, speaking excitedly, their conversation grabbing everyone's attention.

"What's going on?" Christy called out.

"We just broke up a fight. Jimmy Aiken and Brian McCullough."

Gen tensed. Those names she recognized. Brian was Melissa's boyfriend, and she'd dated Jimmy twice before him.

Christy shook her head in mock surprise. "Goodness, I wonder what that could have been about?"

As everyone laughed, Gen turned to Christy. "Melissa?"

Christy sighed. "Yep. Always Melissa."

The taller of the two men who'd announced the news grabbed a paper sack out of the refrigerator and joined them. "When is Jimmy ever going to get it through his head that Melissa isn't going to give him the time of day? The poor kid practically tackled her on the way out of class."

"What happened?"

"They were walking out of History when Joe Kelly dropped a book. Melissa knocked into him, and Jimmy went to the rescue, trying to catch her before she fell." The teacher rolled his eyes. "He put his arms around her, Melissa yelped and Brian went into rescue mode."

"Ugh," Christy said. "Hey, Dave, do you need professional help with the fight? We've got a real live cop here to restore order."

"Thanks for the offer, but no. The last thing anyone in that trio needs is fuel to fan the situation. I told them to cool off. They will," Dave said with an Eddie Haskell–looking smirk. Turning to Gen, he held out a hand. "Hi, Officer Slate. I'm Dave. I teach math down in the catacombs with Cary and Christy. My fifth-period class could give any daytime soap a run for its money."

"Call me Gen." Intrigued in spite of herself, she asked, "So Jimmy grabbing Melissa is what set everyone off?"

Dave glanced at other interested teachers. "Not quite. After Brian pulled Melissa out of Jimmy's arms, Jimmy made a comment about Brian not appreciating her."

Christy put her sandwich down. "Wow."

"Then Brian said Jimmy was just upset because he failed yet again to get Melissa to break up with him."

Dave waggled his eyebrows. "I told you it's better than *As the World Turns.*"

"This bickering has been going on for weeks," Christy explained.

"And it's not getting any better. After Jimmy said that, Brian laid into him, and finally Melissa started crying and ran out of the room. I wasn't sure Cary wanted to get involved, but I had to tell him what was going on since Melissa was in the middle of it."

Even though she felt a little zing at Cary's name, Gen concentrated on the real issue. "What about Brian and Jimmy? What are they like?"

The room erupted in laughter. "Let's just

say it's no surprise that Melissa ended up with Brian," Kevin said. "Jimmy's kind of a live wire."

"I taught his older brother," a man standing near the microwave said. "The whole family's wound too tight."

"Do you think he'd ever do anything illegal?" Gen asked. Maybe Jimmy's hurt feelings were displaying themselves in new ways.

Kevin turned to her in surprise. "The question should really be, do I think he'd do anything illegal *again?*"

"MELISSA, GUYS ARE jerks. Once you understand that, everything will get easier," Cary said that evening. Looking out into his backyard at the four pine trees he and Dean had planted almost ten years ago, Cary wondered where the time had gone. The trees had grown...and so had Melissa's problems. Once upon a time, a bad day for Melissa had meant she'd gotten a splinter.

"Even you?"

"Especially me," he said, pulling her into a hug.

Melissa hiccuped as she slumped next

to him. "I can't believe they got in a fight. Over nothing!"

"It probably wasn't nothing to them." He cast her a sideways glance. "It was over you, right?"

Melissa rolled her eyes. "You know what I mean."

He brushed back a long strand of her thick blond hair. "I do."

"I can't believe Jimmy said all that stuff in front of everybody!"

"He's only thinking about you, Missy."

"I wish he'd stop. He needs to back off, listen to me when I tell him no. I love Brian."

"Jimmy likes you, Melissa, and he doesn't understand why you don't feel the same. I've been in his shoes—it's a frustrating place to be."

"Is that how you were with Ms. Daniels?"

Hearing Kate's name made Cary breathe deep. "Yeah. We weren't serious like you and Brian, but I thought we could be."

"What about with Officer Slate?"

Now it was his turn to be on the defensive. "Why do you ask?"

Seeing she'd found a touchy subject, Melissa's pretty blue eyes gleamed. "There's something between the two of you, Uncle Cary. Everyone can tell."

"Is that right?"

"Uh-huh. Officer Slate blushes and stammers every time she's near you."

Actually, he had noticed the blushing part.

"And you, Uncle Cary, get all tongue-tied."

He couldn't deny it. Their relationship was so mixed up on different levels he was all in knots. "You're right. I like her. I think she likes me, too. But it's complicated. Unfortunately the older you are when you fall in love, the harder it is."

"Maybe," she said with some surprise. "I knew I was in love with Brian when he stayed after basketball practice one day to help me with my geometry homework."

"When was that? You know I could have helped—"

"Uncle Cary! I didn't need *help*. I needed *Brian*." Speculatively she leaned closer. "What do you need?"

He needed his life to go on hold for a

couple of weeks so he could concentrate on nothing but Gen Slate and the way she made him feel.

CHAPTER FOURTEEN

"IT'S THE WEEKEND, Gen," Cary said when he called at eight o'clock on Saturday morning.

After juggling the phone while she struggled to sit up, Gen yawned. "Is there a reason you called me to tell me that?"

"Get up. Let's go canoeing."

Gen's eyes opened wide. "Because?"

"It's sunny, it's almost warm and sharing a canoe will place me in close quarters with you." After a pause, his voice came over the line soft and teasing. "Ever shared a canoe before, Gen?"

She laughed in spite of her sleepiness. "I'll let you know in a little while."

"So it's a yes?"

"Absolutely." Peering at the clock, she said, "When do you want to meet? Around two or three?"

"I don't want to wait that long. Meet me

in one hour next to the running store near the bike trail. We'll walk to Joe's Canoe Shop from there."

One hour? Was he insane? "Cary—"

"I never pegged you as lazy. Get yourself out of bed, Slate."

Who was he calling lazy? "I'll be there."

"Don't forget to bring a bathing suit and a change of clothes, okay? You might need them in case you fall in."

"I'll be ready," she said, snickering as she hung up the phone. *If she fell in.* Please.

Cary must have forgotten that she was a West Virginia girl who wasn't afraid of class-V rapids. She certainly didn't need to be reminded of how to paddle or how to stay in a canoe. But, because she was as eager to be with him as he was with her, she decided to let that secret slide for now. Margaret always said it was good for a woman to have a few secrets.

An hour later, they met next to the trail, fully prepared for their day. Gen and Cary signed waivers, rode an old school bus a few miles to the drop-off place and hiked down a windy path to where their canoe was docked.

Painted bright yellow, it sat on the banks of the Little Miami River, just waiting for them to stop arguing.

"I should definitely sit in the front, Gen," Cary said one more time. "The river is calm, but there are a couple of sections where some small rapids kick in where you need to paddle hard."

There was no way Gen was going to let him tell her what to do. "Don't be quick to judge, Hudson. I'm just as strong as you are."

"But that won't help us if you aren't prepared—"

"Listen, I can canoe," she fairly shouted. "I've been up and down the New River in West Virginia more than a dozen times. Most likely I'm more experienced than you are. So hop in."

Cary raised an eyebrow. "Why didn't you tell me that earlier, before I talked about river safety for twenty minutes?"

She grinned. "Because you seemed to think you knew everything and I knew nothing. I wanted you to realize what a goof you were being."

"I guess I was being a goof," he said with a smile. "I just want you happy."

Just like that, her competitiveness melted. "I am happy."

"Good." He waved to the canoe. "All right, get in then. You lead the way."

She didn't argue with that. In fact, she couldn't resist teasing him a little bit as she stowed her gear in the canoe. "Will your feelings be hurt if you sit behind me while I take the lead?"

After a moment, he grinned evilly. "Not in the slightest. As a matter of fact, I'm going to love having you in front of me."

That little comment just about made her trip on a root sticking out of the bank. Gen saved herself in time and hopped in. Cary pushed their canoe into the river and swung inside expertly. As the gentle current pulled them from shore, Cary got comfortable behind her.

Before she knew it, she was sitting snugly in between his legs, her back against his chest. Although it felt good, she chided, "You know, we don't have to sit so close together. There's plenty of room, probably another foot behind you."

"I disagree, Slate." To her surprise, he pushed her ponytail to one side and kissed her nape. "I think this is exactly how we should be sitting."

Gen dipped her paddle in the water, thinking as they floated that Cary might just have a point. His arms felt strong around her, his lips tempting and sure as he brushed them a little lower along the curve of her shoulder.

As the current propelled them forward, Gen leaned back a little more, enjoying the feel of his hands wrapped around her waist. "I've never canoed like this," she murmured. "It's nice."

"It's very nice."

As a wave of contentment washed over her, Gen closed her eyes for a moment. Suddenly their canoe rocked.

Startled, she popped open her eyes and saw that they were coasting right toward a large boulder jutting out of the water. "Rock! Big rock!" she called out, sounding like an idiot.

Immediately Cary sat up and pushed his paddle into the water. He started rowing backward frantically.

The canoe righted for a split second, then rocked again as Cary scooted away from her. Gen thrust her paddle into the water on the opposite side of the canoe.

That's when it became apparent that their jerky movements were no match for the river. After floating past the boulder, their canoe pitched once, twice, then promptly tipped over.

Gen and Cary landed in the water with a noisy splash.

Quickly he grabbed at the boat with one hand and her with the other. As the icy currents rushed around them, they treaded water, and Gen was thankful they were strong swimmers.

After tossing both paddles into the canoe, Cary said, "You okay?"

"I'm fine, but my ego's been better," she replied with a laugh as she grabbed the side of the canoe, as well. "Maybe I shouldn't have acted so cocky about my abilities."

Once they stabilized the boat, they climbed in. Cary laughed. "I think we should concentrate on rowing from now on."

Too wet to argue, Gen relaxed as Cary

got them back on course. Then, as the canoe floated safely through the current again, she knew there was nowhere else she'd rather be on a Saturday morning.

"Let's do this again real soon," she said.

"Anytime you want, Gen. Anytime at all."

IN BETWEEN HER TIME in Pat Brown's classroom and patrolling the school, Gen did some research into Jimmy Aiken's history. After speaking with several teachers and Jimmy's parents she found out the boy had been involved with a few minor misdemeanors. When he was fourteen, he'd been caught by the police trying to buy cigarettes. Another time, he'd done some underage drinking.

However, by all accounts, the boy had been on the straight and narrow ever since he'd been chosen to be on the varsity basketball squad. Coach Jackson revealed that he'd had more than a few talks with Jimmy about expectations...and consequences.

Now it seemed the only thing bothering the boy was a certain blonde cheerleader who had eyes for someone else. However, although Jimmy had cleaned himself up, it was still possible he was the one responsible for all the recent mischief. Turned out that Coach Jackson hadn't held practices during the afternoon Melissa's tires had been slashed or when Gen's own cruiser had been spray painted.

While keeping Jimmy in mind as a possible suspect, Gen increased her efforts to discover who might be creating so much havoc in the school. In the meantime, she also did her best to fit in.

It was amazing how things *didn't* change as a person got older. Gen still hoped people wanted to sit with her at lunch and still didn't want to be the new girl. Though she and Cary had sat together a few times, Gen knew focusing on her budding relationship while she was on duty wouldn't further the investigation or her position in town. She needed to be clearheaded and alert when she talked to other teachers, and being with Cary made everything else fade into the background.

Luckily she'd made a friend in Christy, as well as a few other women.

Gen had also taken pains to get to know Amy better.

The girl really did need a friend. She looked so sad, so eager for attention, Gen couldn't help but compare herself to her. High school had been hard for Gen, always being in Margaret's shadow. No matter what Gen did, she never seemed to measure up to her sister's beauty, grades or reputation. Though she'd pretended she didn't care, Gen had desperately wanted to be known just as Gen, not as Margaret Slate's little sister.

As they walked down the hall, Amy seemed a little more distant than the last time they'd talked. So far, she'd hardly met Gen's gaze. Instead she focused on her feet.

"Is everything okay?" Gen asked.

"No."

"Anything you want to talk about?"

"Not unless you know how to get my dad to pay attention to me. He was going to take me shopping last night but got home too late."

"My dad was always busy, too." Studying the girl, Gen asked, "Shopping for anything special?"

"Maybe. I…wanted something to wear to the next basketball game."

Gen was surprised. Everyone had been supercasual at the games she'd gone to, just dressed in simple jeans and sweatshirts. "I hope he has time to take you shopping soon."

"I do, too." Amy turned to Gen, her brown eyes looking bigger than usual in her pale face. "Everyone who matters is going to be at the game."

"I guess so. Anyone special you're hoping to see?"

For a moment Gen was sure Amy was going to tell her. But then she shook her head. "Forget I said anything."

"If you need a friend to shop with, I could take you."

Amy rolled her eyes. "I don't think so."

Gen didn't know whether to be amused or offended. "I'll see you later, Amy."

But, once again, Amy had already taken off.

CHAPTER FIFTEEN

"GEN, WAIT UP!" Cary called as she exited the building on Wednesday.

As Gen turned to watch him approach, she smiled. He was loping again, just as he had the first time they'd met. Of course, now she doubted she'd refuse any offer he sent her way. "Hey! How was your day?"

Warmth slid into his eyes. "Good…and on its way to getting better."

Her stomach tightened when she felt his gaze settle on her lips. Oh, it was dangerous for her to be anywhere near Cary Hudson.

Acting as if he hadn't just said anything suggestive, he grinned. "I was going to go pick up Sludge and take him to Paxton Lake Park. He loves it there…lots of trees and statues to inspect. Why don't you bring Sadie along?"

Going to the park sounded good, and

bringing the beagles sounded even better. "Tell me where and when and I'll be there."

After quickly giving her directions, he looked at his watch. "It's four-thirty now. Meet you at the park in thirty minutes?"

"I'll be there."

PAXTON LAKE PARK WAS exactly as Cary had described it. Filled with statues, there were a hundred things for a hound to sniff and explore, making it a beagle paradise.

Comfy in her jogging outfit and tennis shoes, Gen grinned as she spied Cary. Dressed in a torn red sweatshirt, faded cargo shorts and beat-up tennis shoes, he looked as if he'd just crawled out from behind a rock.

He laughed when she told him that. "You, on the other hand, look like you're modeling workout gear."

"Ha-ha."

"Seriously, you look pretty, Gen."

Those simple words brought forth a rush of pleasure.

Gesturing to his own ratty clothes, he said, "I've learned never to wear good clothes while walking Sludge."

"I haven't forgotten our hike, but they seem relaxed and happy today. Sludge seems particularly mild-mannered right now."

"You weren't here the day he spotted a group of rabbits and followed them across a muddy field. Or when he bit though his leash and chased a four-year-old."

"I'm glad I wasn't."

"Oh, he didn't want the kid. Just his ice-cream cone."

Taking a closer look at Sludge, Gen patted Sadie. "Sadie might be constantly hungry, but she's not a menace."

Cary looked skeptical. "Yet." With a motion of his hand, he led the way. Slowly they walked through the park, Cary pointing out various statues and the dates they were dedicated.

The day was glorious. After twenty minutes, Gen pulled off her hooded jacket and tied it around her waist. Sadie and Sludge inspected each other and the statues, but generally minded their manners.

"It sounds like you come here a lot," she observed.

"I do. See the church with the white steeple in the distance? That was my dad's. I spent many afternoons over here while he did 'just one more thing.' Once, Dean and I spent a whole summer here, playing Frisbee baseball. We had a blast."

"Bases were statues?"

"Yep. Almost ran over an old guy sleeping in the sun one day. Scared him half to death. Boy, we got in trouble for that."

His life seemed so quaint. So normal. Easy. Gen wondered if she'd ever felt that connected to her sister or her parents. More often than not she'd spent her time trying to get out from under their scrutiny.

Woof!

Startled by Sludge's sudden deep howl, Gen glanced at the dog in alarm. "I wonder what—"

Woof, woof!

Sadie pulled on her leash as though her life were on the line. In her confusion, Gen lost her grip on Sadie. Unfortunately Sludge pulled away from Cary, too.

Before they knew it, the dogs were off, their leashes trailing behind them like kite tails. They barked madly as they dashed over an expanse of grass, then over a bed of shining daffodils. An elderly lady walking a golden retriever hastily stepped out of their path.

And still they ran.

"Oh, no," Cary muttered. "Look!"

Gen gasped as she saw the dogs' target—two teenagers eating a large pepperoni pizza on the grass.

"They're picnicking!" she yelled, imagining what was coming next.

"They're being attacked," Cary corrected, as with one mighty howl Sludge leaped forward, Sadie at his heels.

Gen groaned.

The two kids yelped in surprise.

Sadie, that beast, howled again.

Sludge just stuck his muzzle in the middle of the pizza pie and opened wide.

Within seconds, the two beagles were chomping as if they'd found nirvana.

Cary reached them first. "Sludge, you horrible animal. What am I going to do with you?"

Sludge burped.

Hastily Cary wrapped the end of the leash around his hand. "Sorry about this, kids," he told the teens.

"Mr. Hudson, your dog sucks. I used my last twenty to buy this," the boy said.

After grabbing Sadie, Gen looked regretfully at the teenagers. "I'm really sorry about your pizza. The leashes slipped."

"The dogs have no manners," Cary finished. Fishing in his pocket, he pulled out a bill. "Brandon, here's twenty dollars to make up for our dogs' deplorable behavior."

"I really am sorry. These dogs...they egg each other on," Gen added. "They also haven't learned to listen."

"They haven't learned to do much," Cary mumbled.

Brandon looked from Gen, then to Cary and back to Gen again. "You're the new cop."

"I am."

With a grin, Brandon cast a sideways glance Cary's way. "Dating, Mr. Hudson?"

The teen's smirk said a thousand words. Cary wasn't inclined to give him any more ammunition for gossip at school. "Maybe."

"How's it going?"

Cary's cheeks began to redden. "My dog just got loose and ate your pizza. So far, pretty good."

Brandon pocketed the money. "No hard feelings."

"Thanks."

The girl laughed. "See ya, Mr. H."

Taking the dogs securely by their leashes, Cary and Gen glanced at each other. "I hadn't planned on this."

"What? Seeing students?"

"The attack of the beagles."

"If you had planned it, I'd be pretty impressed. Not every guy can summon dogs to be completely unruly on command." Now that the adventure was over, Gen threw back her head and laughed. "You trotting over those flowers was the funniest thing I've seen in a long time."

Cary soon joined in. "I thought you were never going to help me. For a moment you looked as stiff as those statues!"

She tried to catch her breath. "Did you see the way Brandon stood in front of his girl?"

"As if he was going to save her from Sludge's vicious appetite." Cary threw an arm around Gen's shoulders as they walked back toward the parking lot. "So...you okay?"

Gen leaned her head on his shoulder. "Other than being a bit unprepared for a 'relaxing' day in the park? I'm fine. Thanks for this. I haven't laughed so hard in ages. It…did me good."

"It did me good, too." He dropped his arm.

She missed his touch already. "So, see you at school tomorrow?"

"Yeah. See you, Slate," he muttered right before he pulled her to him and kissed her.

She wrapped her arms around him, just as Sadie howled again.

CHAPTER SIXTEEN

"AND NOW…I BRING you…the Lane's End Lions!"

The gymnasium walls practically shook as the crowd roared to their feet. Chants and whistles blew as the team entered the gymnasium one member at a time.

After a full minute of applause, Coach Jackson began calling out the starting lineup. Each player stepped forward as the crowd chanted his name.

After standing up and sitting down for about the tenth time, Dave looked at Cary. "This pep rally is nuts! If we have to stand up one more time to sing the fight song, my knees are going to give out."

"Mine, too. All our years of running are taking a toll."

As if on cue, the band started playing again. The crowd dutifully got to their feet, Dave grunting with the effort. As the

Lions' mascot raced out, the fans' shouts reached a higher decibel. "This is crazy!" Dave exclaimed.

Cary had to agree. Not only was the whole student body there, but a large segment of the general population was in attendance to cheer on the Lions, too. Everyone stood together, shoulder to shoulder, waving bright gold-and-black pennants and signs. The band played, the cheerleaders screamed, the crowd whistled and yelled for all they were worth.

Cary figured there was only one person present who wasn't firmly gripped by Lion pride: Gen Slate.

She was easy to spot in the crowd. Clad in her blue uniform, she stood by the main entrance, her mouth conspicuously shut, her eyes continuously scanning the crowd.

She was on duty today to keep the peace. From her strained expression, Cary thought it was pretty obvious that peace was fairly hard to come by. Every few minutes she'd speak into a walkie-talkie. A couple of times, she directed the cheerleaders to stand back or asked people to leave the exits free.

Noticing the direction of his gaze, Dave nudged him. "Officer Slate doesn't look like much of a basketball fan," he said. "I haven't seen her smile yet."

"I think she likes basketball fine. I have a feeling everything else is making her crazy."

"It could be worse. From my point of view, the event looks fairly organized."

Cary had to agree. The pep rally was loud and chaotic, but it was basically under tight control. "At least Jimmy and Brian are behaving themselves," Cary said, nodding to the two star forwards.

"They couldn't be any farther apart and still be on the same team," Dave joked.

That was true. Jimmy and Brian were doing their best to stay a good ten feet from each other. Brian also seemed to be keeping a careful eye on Melissa.

At the moment, Missy was holding a large foam board with the word *ROCK* painted on it, while the band played the perennial Queen favorite "We Will Rock You."

Dave clapped along. "I gotta tell you, I feel as happy as the kids. When was the last time we had a day off for a sporting event?"

That answer was easy. "Never."

"You going to the game tomorrow? Wilmington's about an hour north."

"It's the final game in the division championship to decide who's going to state. Of course I'll be there."

"Taking Gen?"

"If she wants to go."

When the crowd quieted down so Coach Jackson could speak, Cary focused on Gen again. Though she'd probably say he was crazy, he admired how the uniform did incredible things for her figure.

He felt almost proprietary as he watched her. Over and over, she spoke to more people, including a six-year-old who wanted to feel the badge clipped to her hip.

She really was a great cop. She commanded authority even though she was smaller than about half the population in the gym.

As two kids stood nearby and joked with her, Cary realized that she'd accomplished one of her objectives since moving to Lane's End—she'd made friends with a number of the students.

He laughed as a man who blocked the exit faced a very different Gen Slate. She treated him to a glare that would make anyone shake in his boots.

On closer inspection, Cary realized he knew the guy she was chewing out—one of his father's parishioners. Gene Clancy was probably going to think twice before crossing Officer Gen Slate again.

Later that afternoon, after the Lions roared to victory and had officially made it to the finals, the crowds disappeared and the cleanup was well under way, Cary walked Gen out.

"You didn't have to wait for me," she said.

"I wanted to."

"I'm glad." Her eyes sparkling in the bright sunshine as they exited the gym, she said, "I'm getting used to seeing you all the time."

"Me, too." He couldn't resist slipping his hand down her arm, finally linking her fingers with his. "Where are you off to now?"

"I have a gardening lesson."

He didn't even try to hide his surprise. "Of all the activities I picture you doing, gardening isn't one of them."

She laughed. "It's a long story about how it came about, but Bonnie said she had time to help me today. I'm growing lilies."

Because he loved to see her smile, he teased her gently. "Growing lilies? Is that police code for something?"

"You're ridiculous," she countered, flashing him a beautiful grin. "For your information, I planted Easter lilies…but they're not doing well. I'm either giving them too much water or not enough. As of right now, they may be dead by Easter instead of blooming prettily."

Blooming prettily. "I never pictured you as a gardener."

"That's the problem! I'm not."

He squeezed her hand. "How about I stop by later and check up on those lilies?"

"Now you sound like you're the one who's talking in code."

Pausing at her car door, he said, "Maybe I am. Maybe I want to do more than check out your flowers."

"Maybe I'll let you stop by."

The look in her blue eyes made him step a little closer, wrap his arms around her waist…and press his luck. "Tomorrow, how about you let me take you to the game? It's a big one—if we win, we're going to state."

"What do I get if I say yes?"

"Anything you want." Grinning, he leaned toward her, moving close enough to smell a hint of lemon. The tangy scent brought up memories of the other evening when he'd rubbed her back.

Gen looked around. "You're not even thinking of kissing me here, are you?"

"Maybe."

"I'm in my uniform."

"So?"

"So? Cary, that would be a mistake. That would—"

"Be a really good idea," he said quickly.

After all, Cary Hudson might be Lane's End High's favorite teacher. He might have been a preacher's son. He might have been known to have the patience of a saint. But he'd never been one to run from a challenge.

As their lips met, he ran a hand along her

back, loving how right she felt in his arms, how she responded to him, as though what was happening between them was almost too good to be true.

Laughter in the distance pulled them apart.

"I'll come by soon," he said, trying not to let Gen see how much their kiss had affected him, but he was sure he wasn't fooling her for a second. "I'll bring Sludge."

"Can't…wait." She looked dazed.

He nuzzled her cheek. "We can order in. I'll look at your flowers…your lilies."

Gen looked as if she'd forgotten what lilies were.

Just as Cary turned away, he spied two teenagers from his third-period class. "Hi, Kylie. Jason."

Kylie blushed. "Mr. Hudson."

Because they were still staring at him in surprise, he said, "It was a great pep rally, wasn't it?"

Jason laughed. "For some more than others."

Cary couldn't resist agreeing as he unlocked his car.

AN HOUR LATER, GEN stood next to Bonnie and surveyed her four pots filled with lilies. "What do you think?"

Bonnie examined each leaf as though she were the lead detective in a crime lab. Gen found herself holding her breath as she waited to hear the results.

"They're still alive."

Only she would get a landlady who had a real affinity for sarcasm. "Bonnie, even I can tell that. How are they *doing?* Do you think they'll bloom by Easter?"

With a frown, Bonnie stuck a finger in the dirt before rubbing her fingers together. "Maybe."

"I'd hate it if they died before then."

"That would be a real shame."

Oh, good grief. Bonnie might as well have been speaking Greek. So far she hadn't said one meaningful thing. "Thanks for the advice."

"Oh, pish. That's your problem, girl. You're so impatient. You need to learn to curb that, especially when it comes to gardening."

"You need to learn to give me simple directions instead of pitying looks."

"Point taken." With a deep breath, Bonnie issued her proclamation. "The plants... look good."

Gen couldn't believe how happy that made her feel. "Thank you."

"You're welcome. They look so good, in fact, I'm going to let you have a parcel of land right here next to this old oak, where you can design a garden and plant something."

Bonnie's gift was unexpected.

"Get Cary to come out here and help dig and till the soil if need be," Bonnie continued. "He's got a good set of muscles."

"I can dig and till by myself," Gen retorted.

Bonnie started laughing. "Oh, honey. Why would you want to?" She handed her a spade right before she glanced toward Sadie. "That blasted beagle. Look what she's doing, Genevieve."

Gen wished she hadn't since what she saw was disappointing.

Sadie was currently nosing the twenty-pound bag of birdseed Bonnie had bought on sale and Gen had carried to the backyard. Actually, *nosing* was putting it mildly.

Sadie had ripped a three-inch hole in the sack and was currently trying to fit her whole snout and two paws into it.

"Sadie!" Bonnie called out—as if Sadie would listen. "Stop!"

Sadie didn't.

"If you don't, I'm going to tan your hide."

As Sadie ingested a mouthful of seed and chomped down hard, it was extremely evident she couldn't have cared less about Gen's embarrassment.

Bonnie scowled. "That dog is no good."

"She really is a good dog. She's just ruled by her stomach."

Sadie tilted her head as she judged the taste of the seed. Deciding she enjoyed it, she wagged her tail and dug in for more.

"I guess she's fond of sunflower seeds," Gen said.

"She's fond of anything that sits still long enough," Bonnie said with a frown. "You deal with her."

Gen obeyed. "Sadie, you come here now!" she yelled. When Sadie obediently trotted over, Gen turned to Bonnie. "I'll clean up this mess. Thanks for the land, too—I just might use it."

"It would be for you. Not her." Looking madder than a wet hen, Bonnie tromped inside.

Mentally Gen added plastic containers for the birdseed to her grocery list when her cell phone rang.

"I'm picking you up at eight tomorrow morning. We're taking you out to breakfast," Christy said cryptically.

"Huh?"

"It's tradition."

"I'll be ready," Gen said right as Christy clicked off.

"Ready for what?" Cary asked from the fence by the driveway.

Pleased to see him, she pointed to her phone. "Christy just invited me out to breakfast tomorrow."

Cary looked as if that was the funniest thing he'd ever heard. "Did she now? Well, you should have a good time."

"You sound suspicious. What do you know that I don't?"

"Enough."

Like a kid, he hopped the fence before stepping out of the way to let a patient

Sludge in through the gate. Sadie barked in greeting.

As the dogs started chasing each other and destroying even more of the birdseed sack, Cary strode to her side. "Are these your lilies?"

"Yep."

"They look good."

"Oh, stop. They just look green."

"Actually, I'd say everything looks very good."

With a start, Gen noticed he was no longer looking at plants. Nope, instead it seemed Cary only had eyes for her.

Gen felt as if a jumble of bees had come out to play in her stomach. All the feelings that had sprung up during their last kiss had surfaced again, making her feel wonderful and excited and nervous.

All she could think about was the feel of his lips.

"So...I've looked at your plants."

Indeed he had. "And you brought Sludge to play."

He glanced at their beagles. Now Sludge was doing his best to eat more seed than

Sadie. "They seem happy." Pulling her close, he said, "Now I get what I want."

"Which is?"

"You, Gen Slate. All I want to do at this very moment is kiss you again."

"Thank goodness. It feels as if it's been forever."

Cary grinned just before he claimed her mouth one more time. "You're right. At least an hour."

CHAPTER SEVENTEEN

"I FEEL LIKE I'm back in high school," Gen said to the four women she was sitting at the table with at the Waffle Shack on Main.

"You are, in a way," Christy countered.

"I suppose, though only until this vandalism case is solved."

"That's true, but we like you anyway." Christy soaked up a piece of French toast in a pond of butter and syrup before replying, "You should feel special—we don't kidnap just every new girl."

"Do you always pick up your guests two hours early?"

The women looked at each other and smiled. "Always."

Remembering how shocked she'd been to see Christy, Jill, Monique and Beth surrounding her bed, Gen shook her head. "I can't believe you got in without Sadie or me knowing about it."

Monique winked. "Bonnie helped with Sadie."

"We love that we put one over on a cop." Christy grinned. "Come on, admit it, this is fun, don't you think?"

It had been fun, from the time the women had appeared at her house at six this morning, to the giggles they'd shared when Bonnie had yelled out the window to settle down as they got on their way to the Waffle Shack.

But Gen wasn't quite ready to give in so easily. "Oh, it's been terrific—if you forget about the fact that I'm out in public in pajama bottoms, a sweatshirt and no makeup."

Jill put down her coffee cup. "Of course you had to bring that up. We took a vote and have decided that we don't like you anymore. No one should look so good first thing in the morning."

Gen laughed. "Thanks."

The conversation rolled on. Before she knew it, Gen was commenting on reality TV shows, the newest celebrity gossip, how to make the best banana bread and the chances of Lane's End actually winning the state championship.

All the women seemed interested in what she had to say and, even more special, were talking as if this morning was the first of many breakfasts to be shared.

Gen was loving every minute of it.

She didn't know why she was so surprised. Maybe because she'd always assumed most other girls had a secret club that she couldn't be a part of?

How wrong she'd been! And how she couldn't wait to call Margaret and tell her what she'd been doing. Though she had a feeling her sister would say the morning sounded exactly like something Gen would enjoy, she had a feeling her sister would also be sensitive enough to comment on how good it had been for Gen to venture even further from her self-imposed shell.

Later, after their dishes were cleared away and a third pot of coffee consumed, all four women peered at Gen regretfully.

"Here's the part where we make you pay for the meal," Beth said, not a gleam of humor in her eyes.

It was a small price to pay for everything she'd gained. "Okay."

The girls whooped it up again. "We're teasing." Jill laughed. "We'd never make you buy breakfast."

"Unless you want to twist our arms," Christy said.

"I'd pay for breakfast if it means we can get together again," Gen said, meaning every word.

Monique squeezed her hand. "That goes without saying."

"Well, then, thanks."

"You're welcome," Monique replied before turning to the others with an exaggerated grimace. "It's really too bad Cary couldn't see you like this, all dressed up in your bedtime finery. He wouldn't know what hit him."

"Cary and I have gotten pretty close... but not this close," she said, fingering her T-shirt.

"You two have looked pretty close to me," Jill said. "Monique and I saw you two kissing in the parking lot."

Gen hadn't counted on an audience. "You saw us?"

"*Everyone* saw you."

Gen grimaced. "I thought most people had already gone home."

"Even if someone had wanted to give you privacy, it would've been practically impossible to do—considering Cary looked like he was holding on to you for dear life."

Beth nudged Jill as she teased, "Was it a life-or-death matter, Gen? Were you giving him mouth-to-mouth?"

Gen blushed. "I don't know what happened. Some things between us get intense. One minute I'm talking to Cary, the next I'm kissing him like there's no tomorrow."

Christy whistled. "No tomorrow, huh?"

Monique fanned herself. "Ooh, honey. You've got it bad."

"I...well, all things being equal, please don't tell him I sleep with a mouth guard."

Beth's eyes twinkled. "We wouldn't dare."

Gen pointed at her dog pajamas, the ones she'd bought when Sadie was a puppy. They also happened to be frayed at the edges and two inches too short. "Better not mention these, either."

Christy raised three fingers in a mock salute. "Scout's honor."

"And—"

"Don't say another word, Gen," Cary called from behind her. "Take it from me—these ladies already have enough ammunition to make my life a nightmare."

"Oh, come on, Cary," Monique whined. "We were just getting started."

He lifted one brow significantly.

Gen closed her eyes in mortification. Like an old Bugs Bunny cartoon character, she turned her head slowly, hoping that she'd just imagined what was really happening. No such luck.

There was Cary, standing a mere four feet behind her, looking good, as always, in faded jeans and a worn button-down shirt.

It was too bad he looked as if he was about to crack up. And why not? Every woman who had kidnapped her was practically on the floor laughing.

Gen was completely embarrassed. "Please tell me you didn't hear this conversation."

"I can't do that."

Mentally she reviewed everything she'd

just tossed out of her mouth like trash from a fast-food restaurant. Kissing? No tomorrow? Closing her eyes, she whispered, "Mouth guard?"

"Heard that."

"Pajamas?"

His gaze ran over her like a hit-and-run. "Yep."

She gave in to curiosity. "Kissing?"

"I listened real closely to that part." As the women at the table giggled, he pointed out, "It did have to do with me, you know."

Everything she'd said had to do with him. For weeks he'd been on her mind.

Practically 24-7.

Since she had nothing but pride left, she kicked out a leg. "So what do you think of my pajamas?"

Crouching next to her, he studied the flannel fabric covering her legs. "I love them."

Gen didn't know which was more humiliating—that he knew she wore dog pajamas to bed or that he could make her feel completely attractive wearing them.

Right now nothing seemed more appealing than the way he was looking at her, all languid brown eyes and amusement.

"Oh, Cary, you're in deep trouble," Christy called out. "She's got you good."

Gen begged to differ. She didn't really *have* him.

But then Cary slid his fingers through hers, linking them, letting her know without a word that he still found her cute. "She does, Christy. It's the truth."

Gen gasped.

After a brief squeeze, Cary stood up. "I'm going to get you out of here," he murmured.

"I think that's a great idea."

Turning to the women, he said, "We'll see you later."

"It's about time you took her away," Christy teased.

Leaning in to Cary, Gen whispered, "Did you plan this breakfast?"

He gestured around the tiny diner. "No. If I was going to treat you to breakfast, I'd have done better than this."

"So you didn't know they were going to kidnap me?"

"I knew they were going to take you

out—at least I hoped they would. This breakfast is an initiation ritual of sorts, and it seems you've passed with flying colors. I counted on them taking you to the Waffle Shack. There aren't too many places that serve breakfast in Lane's End."

He chuckled as he grabbed her coat from the rack near the entrance and slipped it around her shoulders. "I don't think I'll ever forget your expression when you saw me standing there. Too funny."

As they walked out the front door, Gen looked back at the women, who were pouring another round of coffee and chatting. Even if Cary hadn't come to rescue her—and she was very glad he had—she was happy to be part of the club.

Cary opened the front door and slipped an arm around her shoulders as they walked to his SUV. "I'm glad I came when I did. Rumor has it they made Monique go shoe shopping at the mall—for six hours. She said she ended up spending $400 on shoes with four-inch heels. No telling what you would've come home with."

"I couldn't handle heels like that."

"I don't know how anyone could—

though, to be honest, I wouldn't mind seeing those legs of yours in high heels. You've got great legs." He quickly held up a hand. "Sorry, am I being completely chauvinistic?"

She grinned. "A little."

"Sorry," he said again, but he didn't look especially apologetic.

After they hopped in his truck, she turned to him. "So you think I have nice legs?"

"I think you have nice everything." Before he started the car, he pulled her closer. "I can't help myself when it comes to you. Every time I see you, I want to hold you close, kiss you senseless."

She knew that feeling well. As their lips met, she felt his hands glide along her back. She crossed her arms behind his neck and luxuriated in his attention.

Could anyone on earth kiss as well as Cary Hudson?

Gen lost track of time, of where she was and who she was. All she wanted was for the moment to never end.

Cary didn't seem to care about anything but kissing her. Finally, though, he pulled away.

He leaned back and buckled up. "I'd better get you home. I'm sure you'd like to shower and get dressed."

She nodded.

They drove a few miles before he spoke again. "This is probably going to sound ridiculous, but I want you to know I'm serious about you, Gen."

Once again she was astounded at how Cary could share his feelings so openly. Her insecurities always got the best of her, and she couldn't bring herself to speak her mind.

She'd learned to censor her emotions growing up with her mom, and her relationship with Keaton had cemented the habit. Only a fool would open herself up to the possibility of ridicule or misunderstanding.

Yet she felt the same way as Cary. She was serious about him, too.

So why couldn't she tell him how she felt?

Her silence filled the car.

"That's what I was afraid of," he murmured.

"I do like being with you, Cary," she said.

"You do?" He took a deep breath. "Next weekend, if the Lions win regionals, they'll be at the state tournament in Columbus. If you want, we could go together and stay overnight. You'd have your own room," he was quick to assure her.

She had to smile at his thoughtfulness.

Her answer was simple. "I want."

Cary turned down her street and pulled up next to her Outback. Pleasure lit his eyes. "Yeah?"

"Yeah."

Before she could say anything else, Cary claimed her lips one more time. She responded wholeheartedly, feeling better about their future.

Sadie's bark from the fence drew her away.

"See you later?" Cary asked as she got out of his truck.

"You will. Good luck with that mulch."

He flashed her a smile. "Go back to bed, Slate. I'll call you later."

After his Explorer pulled out of the driveway, she slowly walked upstairs, Sadie running beside her impatiently. "What a morning," she said to the dog as she unlocked the door and stepped inside her living room.

As Sadie trotted to her bedroom to nap, Gen found she couldn't follow. She was too keyed up, her mind spinning over her conversation with Cary.

Why hadn't she been able to tell him how special she thought he was? That she was falling in love with him? That she loved how considerate he was, how caring he was to everyone around him?

How he made her feel as if she was worth his time, his attention, his love?

But she was scared. What if she froze and couldn't deliver the words he was looking for?

Or, even worse—what if she did open up and bare her soul and was found wanting?

What would she do then?

CHAPTER EIGHTEEN

THE FOLLOWING WEEK passed in a whirlwind. Gen spent the days patrolling the school and talking to kids. Luckily there hadn't been another vandalism incident, which Evan attributed to her presence.

Gen was glad that the principal saw her being there as a plus, but truthfully she wasn't sure whether she was doing much good or not. She'd ruled out Jimmy as a suspect, which left Amy as her prime suspect, and Gen still had plenty of misgivings about that. While Amy did, indeed, have large blocks of time unaccounted for and a witness seemed to remember seeing Amy buy spray paint, Gen didn't have the proof she needed to accuse her of the vandalism and frankly, didn't want to believe she was responsible.

Gen had gotten to know the girl pretty well. Amy hadn't displayed any tendencies toward violence that Gen had observed, though she did seem infatuated with Brian McCullough and was somewhat jealous of Melissa. Gen kept careful documentation of her conversations with Amy, hoping against hope that something would stand out and give Gen a reason to confront the girl…or cross her off as a potential suspect.

On a more positive note, Gen had been spending a lot of time lately with Cary. They'd had lunch together twice and had spent every evening either at his place or hers.

Each night, it had been harder and harder to say goodbye. But she knew that at some point he'd want to talk about their relationship. By the time Cary picked her up on Friday at five, she was a bundle of nerves.

IF CARY NOTICED SHE was tense during the two-hour drive to Columbus on I-71, he didn't let on. For most of the way, all he talked about was the game, Coach Jackson's game plan for the upcoming state tournament and assorted other high school business.

"The cheerleaders are staying together in

rooms chaperoned by three moms," he said as they got closer to the stadium. "If Melissa even so much as thinks about drinking, smoking or sneaking out, they'll know about it."

Gen was surprised Cary was worried. "Melissa seems awfully levelheaded to me. I'd be shocked to hear she did any of those things."

"It would surprise me, too, but I have to remember that she's a normal teenager going on an overnighter. And, well, sometimes things happen."

Cary took the next exit, circling around the Ohio State campus until they arrived at Easton Plaza, a ritzy shopping area north of Columbus.

"The Hilton is here," he said simply, exiting the ramp and parking in the guest area.

"I'm glad we're not staying near the kids."

"You and me both. Luckily we get to be avid basketball fans, not chaperones."

While Cary brought in their bags and registered at the front desk, Gen stood to the side, finding it easy—for the first time—to let someone else be completely in charge.

When they exited the elevator, he nodded before leading the way to their rooms. He slipped in the key card and opened her door.

Gen looked around in appreciation. Dominating the room was a king-size bed piled high with down comforters, pillows and crisp white sheets. "This is lovely."

Taking her hands, he pulled her into his arms. Gen rested her head on his chest. Felt his heart beating.

Running his hand along her spine, he said, "You're smart yet unsure. So brave yet so delicate." He chuckled. "You've had me running in circles, hoping to please you, afraid to scare you away. Wanting to tell you how I felt but worried it was too soon."

"You make me sound weak."

"We both know you're not that. But it's okay to be vulnerable every now and then."

She swallowed. "You're right."

"Glad to see you're agreeing with me so easily."

She looked up at him. "At first I was afraid to let you know how I felt because the last guy who was this nice to me only wanted me as a friend."

"That was his loss."

Feeling so comfortable, listening to his heart beat while he held his arm around her, she took a risk. "Cary...what about Kate?"

KATE.

Just thinking about her made his stomach twist into knots. "I don't want to talk about Kate right now."

But Gen didn't let it go. "She's a beautiful woman."

So was Gen. Cary ran a hand along her arm. He wanted to hold her close forever.

"Cary?"

He forced himself to still his hand. "It wasn't like this, Gen. I thought I was in love with her, but now I realize I just wanted to be in a relationship."

Cary tried to guess what she was thinking. But all he could see on her face was confusion.

Because of that, he knew he had to keep dredging up old hurts and feelings. "We were both single, had things in common. She was attractive."

Cary shook his head. "But it was never right." He looked into her face. "She wasn't you. She and I weren't *us*." He lowered his voice. "What we had pales in comparison to this."

Pleasure lit Gen's lapis-blue eyes, which made Cary light up, too. "Can we stop talking now?" he asked and kissed her quickly before she could say another word.

Cary felt a peace he hadn't felt since before his parents died. Finally his future was settling into place. What he and Gen had was real and strong, as strong a relationship as he'd ever hoped to attain. He had no doubts about them, only a perfect sense of calmness.

CHAPTER NINETEEN

"R-E-B-O-U-N-D!" MELISSA AND the rest of the cheerleaders yelled out. "Rebound that ball!"

Brian McCullough missed the shot. The point guard from the Pacers grabbed the ball, dribbled down the court and scored two more points.

Green-and-white banners swung madly in the air. Bells and whistles sounded. Fans from Lane's End groaned.

The score was now 35-22. The Lions were doing their best, but it was obvious to everyone in the stadium that they weren't going to win the state championship. From the first dribble, the team from Toledo seemed to tower over their tallest kids. They passed and shot and played better.

As the action began again, Dave whistled low. "Ouch," he murmured to Cary and

Gen. "That forward stole the ball without so much as a 'Have a nice day.'"

As Jimmy's pass to fellow teammate Gideon Young fell short, Cary nodded. "It's getting ugly."

Dean, who sat two rows down, glanced up at Cary. "Brian doesn't look too good."

No, he didn't. The star forward's face was flushed and he looked out of breath. Perspiration soaked his hair.

As the Pacers scored again, Brian shook his head in frustration.

In the stands, Cary did his best to be optimistic. "It's not over yet. They still have a shot."

But as the third quarter melted into the fourth, it was a forgone conclusion. The Lions were going to lose.

When the final buzzer sounded, the score was Pacers 46, Lions 38.

As the Pacers drenched their coach in Gatorade and cheered their victory, half the Lions had tears in their eyes. Some folks in the crowd did, too.

On the court, Melissa was hugging Brian, all six-foot-two sweaty inches of him. Her arms were wrapped around his neck, tears openly trailing down her cheeks. Brian whispered something that made her smile as the rest of the team slapped one another on the back.

As they made their way out of the stands, Cary nudged Dean. "Look at Melissa."

"She loves that kid," her father said. "It's pretty obvious he feels the same way."

Cary smiled as Brian kissed Melissa's brow before joining his teammates.

After waiting a beat, Dean strode down the bleachers' metal steps and signaled his daughter over.

Gen, who'd been talking to Christy and a couple of other teachers, linked arms with Cary. "They were so close to winning. I feel so sorry for those boys."

"Me, too."

A CROWD GATHERED AT the front entrance of the stadium, far more subdued than at any other time this season, a few people half-heartedly waving wrinkled banners and signs as they watched the basketball team load their bus. When it pulled out, the remaining spectators valiantly cheered the boys one more time before dispersing.

"What are you guys up to now?" Christy asked.

"Melissa's riding home with the team, so I'm going to go check out of the hotel," Dean said.

Cary turned to Gen. "Ready to head back home?"

She nodded.

As she walked next to Cary toward the parking lot, a dozen emotions swam through her: disappointment for the team, weariness as the excitement of the past couple of days caught up to her and happiness because she felt as if she and Christy had forged a friendship.

But overriding everything else was contentment. She and Cary were getting to be a real couple. It was so nice to be able to concentrate on the present and not have to worry about the past anymore. And as far as the future...well, that would take care of itself.

Once they were alone in the truck, Cary slapped his hand against the steering wheel. "What a bummer. It would have been so cool if they'd won."

"It would have been," she agreed. "Luckily our weekend wasn't a total loss."

When he turned to her, warmth lit his eyes. "Last night was wonderful." Although they'd had separate rooms, they'd spent several hours kissing and talking about their lives and dreams.

She sighed. "Yes, it was."

He started the engine and pulled out onto the highway. Gen leaned her head back against the headrest, already imagining being in his embrace as soon as they reached Lane's End. Hopefully, they could spend most of Sunday together, too.

Cary turned on a classic-rock station and they sang along to the Eagles as the Explorer zipped down the highway.

After the last chorus of "Hotel California," Cary cleared his throat. "Maybe tomorrow we can get together and talk about how to handle things from now on."

Tomorrow? Gen turned to him. "Why tomorrow? Are you busy tonight?"

"Well, no."

Warning signals rang in her ears. "You don't want to spend more time together?"

"Of course I do, but I'd rather wait until

we decide how to explain our relationship to Melissa."

"Melissa? Why does it matter what she thinks?"

He chuckled, but the laughter sounded strained. "Because I've practically raised her. Because Dean and I have been talking to her about relationships for the last month. I'd rather have us both on the same page, if you know what I mean."

"I don't. What we have is completely different than what goes on between two kids in high school," she retorted, feeling her confidence slipping. What *did* they have?

"I'm not disputing you. I completely agree that our circumstances are different than any teenager's."

"Cary, we're adults."

"Look, this isn't the right time." He ran a hand through his hair. "I'm sorry I brought this up now. Maybe we should wait—"

"We've got this whole drive. Cary, what are you trying to say?"

"That it's important to me to be able to tell Melissa that we're serious about each other. I mean, obviously you know how much I love you."

"What?"

He flicked a wary glance her way. "I thought you understood what I was talking about last week when I said I was serious about you."

He reached for her hand. "I thought you felt the same way. I'm completely, totally in love with you, Gen. I can't wait to see where this goes."

Cary was moving too fast.

Did she love him? She thought she did but wasn't sure. Old fears of laying out her heart, only to get it stomped on, came rushing back. She was afraid to lose him…but now she was just as afraid to lose herself.

At her continued silence, he laughed, the noise bitter and despondent. "Well, that went over real well."

Gen winced and backpedaled, fast. "Maybe we could keep our relationship private for a while."

"That's going to be pretty hard to do. Everyone knows we went to Columbus together."

"But all we did was kiss."

He very carefully pulled his hand from hers. "What did last night mean to you?"

Everything. It meant everything. But she was afraid to admit that. "It was great." Gen was glad it was dark inside the truck's cab; she hoped it concealed her blush.

Because the night before had been so much more than that.

The tender way he'd held her in his arms and their sweet kisses had made her want to forget all her silly worries and agree to anything he wanted.

But she still wasn't sure. Desperately she tried another tack. "Don't forget, I've still got the investigation at school to worry about."

He looked irritated. "I hadn't forgotten."

"Good. Because that's what is important to me." She rushed on, tripping over her words to try to get him to understand. "I do have a lead. I've been taking everything slow—mainly because I didn't want to make a mistake but also because I've enjoyed spending time at the high school so much."

She closed her eyes in a futile effort to calm herself. "What I'm trying really badly to say is…I'm close to finishing up this case."

"You want to hold off on our relationship until after you close the case?" In the dim light Gen watched his jaw tighten.

His anger made her desperate. She tried again. "I know it means we'll have to take things one step at a time, but well, that's what we have been doing."

Cary's grim expression didn't change.

Had she ever seen him look so harsh? She made one last attempt to explain. "What I'm trying to say is…nothing has to change."

"It already has, Gen."

"Well, I don't like how you're pushing me toward a public commitment. I told you I'm not great at relationships."

"What happened to everything we talked about?"

"I'm just asking you to go slow."

He ran a hand through his hair. "I don't believe it. What is it with me? This is almost the exact thing that happened with Kate. After we got close, she broke up with me."

Now Gen was angry. "I'm not breaking up with you and I'm nothing like Kate. You're overreacting."

"I don't think so."

"That's not fair. You can't bring your old relationship into this. What's happening between us is entirely different."

"Don't talk to me about fairness." He tightened his grip on the steering wheel. "And don't sit here and tell me that the only thing you're worried about is my hangups. Yours are just as much of a problem as mine."

"I guess we have nothing more to say."

"I guess not."

Slumping in her seat, Gen cursed the fact that Columbus was two solid hours north of Lane's End. They had ninety more minutes to get through before she could cry or find some other outlet for her grief.

With a sharp flick of the switch, Cary turned up the volume on the radio. An old Steely Dan song filled the cab as he sped down the highway.

After ten minutes, it was obvious neither one was going to say another word.

After another five, Gen pretended to fall asleep.

CHAPTER TWENTY

IT WAS RAINING when Gen woke up after noon on Sunday. The dreary weather suited her mood just fine. At the moment, her future looked bleak.

Cary's anger had been hurtful. Last night, as the miles had passed and she'd pretended to sleep, she'd used the time to think about her hopes and fears and to imagine how she might have handled things differently. She knew she could've explained herself better, but she wasn't the only one to blame. Cary should have been more patient.

The phone rang. Although every part of her was screaming to ignore it, duty won over.

"Hello? Slate here."

"Gen, I've got news."

Sam's voice was jubilant; there really was no other word for it. She sat up. "What's up?"

"Amy Blythe admitted to the vandalism when I paid her a call this morning."

Instead of feeling happy, the news only made Gen feel even worse. "What? You saw her without me?"

"Amy's English teacher contacted me Friday night. She was grading papers and came across a poem Amy had written. It was practically a confession, Gen. I took it right to Lieutenant Banks."

She was amazed that all of this had happened without her knowing. "Why didn't anyone contact me?"

"You weren't on the clock."

"But this was my case." Gen closed her eyes in frustration. She should have concentrated on work instead of messing up her life in Columbus.

"Why are you upset? Didn't you ask for this weekend off?"

"I'm not upset with you. I guess I'm just disappointed I wasn't there when you spoke to Amy."

"Actually, I think it was good you weren't. Amy indicated she had formed a friendship with you. It might have been harder for her to admit everything with you standing there."

So much for her efforts to befriend the girl. Not only had she not helped Amy, but Gen's actions had hindered her ability to solve the case. Swallowing back personal concerns, she forced herself to be a professional. "What did she say?"

"The kid has some serious emotional issues. Seems she's been fixated on Cary and Melissa for a while. She's jealous of Melissa, of her relationship with Cary and her popularity at school. It appears Amy has the hots for Brian McCullough big-time, too."

"I'm surprised she didn't go to Columbus to watch the game then."

"Her father wouldn't let her, which made her go off the deep end. She was angry and frustrated. When I showed her the poem, she lost it."

"But why spray paint Kate's wall? And my car?"

"It seems she has some kind of hero worship for Cary Hudson. She damaged Kate's wall when she thought Kate wasn't being nice to Cary. And she trashed your car when she thought you were getting too close."

Gen felt sick. "What did Amy's dad have to say?"

"Not a lot. He's having a really hard time with it. I guess financially they've been having some problems, so he's been working overtime, which means Amy's been spending even more time alone."

"Where is she now?"

"Home."

"Maybe I should go talk with her?"

"There's no time. We have roll call in an hour. Sergeant Conrad wanted me to ask you if you'd be willing to report back early. He wants to speak with you ASAP."

IN A DAZE, GEN SAT through roll call, only half listening to the list of petty crimes committed over the past twelve hours. After they were dismissed, Conrad signaled her to his office.

Lt. Banks was already there. "Close the door, Slate," he said when she appeared.

Obediently Gen clicked the door shut behind her and stood at attention, waiting for them to tell her that she'd failed miserably.

For someone who had had so much experience on the streets of Cincinnati, she'd not only *not* solved the case but she'd been out of town when another officer had. She felt worse than a rookie on her first beat.

Conrad playfully nudged her shoulder. "What's with the stance, Officer? Have a seat."

Gen looked at both senior men. Neither appeared especially grim, which struck her as odd. Never one to let bad news come to her, she chose to be proactive.

"I spoke with Sam this morning," she said, giving credit where it was due. "He told me about Amy. That was good work."

Sergeant Conrad nodded. "It was. I'm glad he took your lead and ran with it. The captain heard from a couple of people from the city council on Friday. They wanted things settled at the school, fast."

Gen didn't know what else to say. Should she apologize for taking time off? Warily she looked to the lieutenant, who was examining a stack of papers. Deciding to play it safe, she sat still, mouth shut.

After what seemed like an eternity, Lt. Banks looked up. "I've spent quite a bit of time going over your reports from the high school, Gen."

Had she done something else wrong? "Yes, sir?"

"You did a thorough, commendable job."

She knew a "but" was forthcoming. "Yes?"

Conrad chuckled. "This is where you say, 'Thank you,' Slate."

Dutifully she opened her mouth to speak.

But the lieutenant silenced her with a hand. "That's not necessary." He shuffled the papers again. "In his report, Evan wrote that you made a concerted effort to get to know the staff members and student body."

"I did."

He cleared his throat. "In fact, Evan said you bonded so well with the staff that they're going to miss you when you leave."

Gen bit her lip and willed herself to keep calm.

"We'd like you to continue in community relations."

"Sir?"

"Mike Chambers has been our community relations officer for five years. His fluency in Spanish has him working more and more with other departments throughout the city. We'd like you to pick up some of his hours."

That sounded like a promotion. "Excuse me?"

"Effective immediately, we'd like you back on patrol fifty percent of the time and working with Mike the other half." The lieutenant leveled a look her way. "How does that sound to you?"

She wasn't getting fired. She wasn't under investigation for failing to apprehend Amy in a more timely manner. No one was angry at her for taking personal time.

Far from that, she was receiving commendations and being given a promotion. "It sounds good, sir."

Conrad crossed his arms over his chest. "Most people in my experience smile when they're told they're doing a good job, Slate."

Gen grinned, relief filling her. "I'm doing my best not to fall on the floor. I was pretty certain I was being called to account for my weekend."

Lt. Banks tilted his head. "Why? You were clocked off, Gen."

"Sam took up the slack."

"That's what he was supposed to do."

"But…he solved the case."

"Using *your* notes and interviews. We work as a team around here. It's not winner take all."

Conrad gestured toward the door. "Spend the week finishing your business at the high school, then come back and fill out your paperwork. I told Mike you could meet with him first shift on Thursday…if that works for you."

"That works just fine." Gen fought to maintain her self-control. At last, she'd done something right. She was seen as a team player and respected. "Thank you for this opportunity."

"You're welcome, Gen."

With a brief nod, she exited the room. Waved at Sam, who was waiting to get the lieutenant's signature on a stack of paperwork. Checked her schedule once more. Grabbed a headset. Strode to her vehicle.

When she noticed she was alone in the parking lot, she grinned broadly. Things were terrific. Wonderful. Moving to Lane's End had been the best thing she'd ever done.

It was only as she was pulling out of the parking lot that she remembered.

Cary.

Just like that, Gen realized she hadn't done a thing right after all.

THREE DAYS PASSED and Cary still hadn't spoken to Gen.

Three long, miserable, pointless days.

He'd picked up the phone several times to call her and apologize, but, with one exception, he'd hung up before she'd answered.

The one time he'd stayed on the line, he'd heard her sweet, husky voice on the machine and had closed his eyes.

He'd been such a fool.

What had he been thinking? He'd blown everything out of proportion and made Gen choose between her job and her private life. He'd been so afraid of being hurt again that he'd messed up something great.

What was even worse, she hadn't even been trying to break up with him; she'd just wanted time.

The past few days had taught him several lessons. He needed to apologize and he needed her back. He was going to do whatever it took to make it up to her. Flowers? A gold bracelet?

No, those weren't really her style.

But a puppy was.

Cary smiled at the thought. Yeah, a new beagle puppy and a sincerely worded apology ought to do the trick. He needed Gen in his life. He hoped one day she'd feel the same.

"WHAT ARE WE GOING TO talk about now, Mr. Hudson?" Aaron Kanz said during the end of sixth period on Friday. "Basketball's over."

Aaron was right. After months of discussing everything from the Lions' chances of winning to the NCAA championship, talking about anything else seemed anticlimactic.

"Cross-country running? Tennis?" When Aaron groaned, Cary waited two beats. "Algebra?"

That got more than a few kids to smile, which suited Cary just fine. It had been hard to think about anything but going to state. The excitement of the basketball season combined with the stress from the vandalism and his relationship with Gen had exhausted him.

Bells chimed, signaling the end of class and the end of the week. Cary sat down as the students filed out. After spending the next hour marking papers and entering the grades into the computer, he intended to take a long and hopefully cathartic run with Sludge.

"Hey, Mr. Hudson?"

Cary stood up when he saw Amy Blythe standing at the door. "Come in, Amy. This is a surprise."

She looked behind her and Cary saw her dad standing there. "You, too, Roger. Have a seat."

He shook his head. "Thanks, but Amy wanted to do this on her own."

Amy hesitantly stepped forward. "I just wanted to say I was sorry."

Cary had been keeping up with what was happening with Amy after she'd confessed. She'd been expelled from Lane's End High instead of facing criminal charges. In return, her father had agreed to take her for counseling and enroll her in a private school for troubled teens.

He felt for the Blythes. Both were going to be dealing with the consequences of Amy's actions for years to come.

Cary held out his hand and clasped Amy's gently. "I'm glad you stopped by." And because she needed to hear it, he said sincerely, "I forgive you for what you did."

Her eyes widened. "That's it?"

"That's it. Everyone makes mistakes."

Amy gave him a half smile and walked toward the door. "See ya."

Cary waved before going over to his whiteboard. Seeing Amy reminded him again of how much he missed Gen. He hoped one day soon they, too, could—

"Hey. Am I interrupting anything?"

For a moment Cary was sure his heart had stopped. He shook his head. "Gen."

"Hi. I had to stop by...needed to tie up some loose ends." She flipped her ponytail over one shoulder. "Did you see Amy?"

"I did."

Gen smiled. "I'm going to be her mentor. I...I didn't want her to think I was only pretending to be her friend."

"She wouldn't. That's not your style."

"No, it's not." Without asking, Gen pulled up a chair and sat down. "Can we talk?"

"Always." Cary perched on the end of his desk.

"I said goodbye to most of the kids on Tuesday, so this is pretty much my last day." Glancing into the hallway, she murmured, "It feels strange." Turning to look at him again, Gen continued. "Believe it or not, I've been feeling a little bit sad about leaving this school. I feel like I belong here."

"You do. Christy and the others...everyone really likes you." He hesitated for a moment before telling her, "I tried to call you."

Her cheeks flushed. "You did?"

"Well, I almost called you. I've been racking my brain for a way to get you to forgive me." He didn't dare mention the puppy—he wanted to give it to her when he was sure the time was right.

"I almost called you, too." Reaching out her hand, she said, "I'm so sorry about the other night."

"No, it was my fault." He shook his head. "I should never have pushed you so much. All I can say is that I had hoped what we had was going to grow into something long-lasting."

Her eyes widened and she opened her mouth, though no sound came out. "I don't do temporary," she said. "I never thought of us like that."

"I never did, either."

"When you started talking about love and commitment, I was afraid to say too much...I was worried I'd say the wrong thing."

"I hardly gave you the opportunity, I was so concerned about my own agenda. But I'm ready to listen now, Gen." He linked his hand with hers.

She stared at their entwined fingers. "I am, too." She took a deep breath. "I've been promoted to working with Mike Chambers in Community Relations. It's...it's a good thing."

"Congratulations." Cary was happy for her—no matter what happened between them, he'd always feel that she was a great cop.

"Thanks. Now that the case here is solved, there's no conflict of interest anymore."

Cary squeezed her hand as he dared to hope. "None that I can see."

She sighed and stepped away as though she still needed a little space. "I just wanted you to know…if you do ever want to call me again, I'd pick up the phone. I like you, Cary. I think I was starting to fall in love with you."

He knew he had fallen. Hard. Now he wondered how he was going to be able to get back up. "I was, too," he murmured.

But she didn't hear him—she'd already turned and was walking away.

As her footsteps faded, Cary straightened his pile of papers, looked across the room at the empty desks. Though things weren't perfect between them, there was promise.

Right then, it was enough.

CHAPTER TWENTY-ONE

GEN'S LILIES HAD grown a good seven inches. The leaves were green and healthy.

Yet there wasn't a bloom to be found.

Bonnie frowned at the plant she held in her hands before turning to Gen. "Easter's next week. With you in charge, I'd say it's gonna be a toss-up whether any of these plants flower or not."

"Thanks for the vote of confidence."

"Anytime," Bonnie groused with a shake of her head.

"I've been doing everything the garden expert told me to do—partial shade, water every other day, plant food."

As Sadie barked at a pesky robin, Bonnie fingered a shiny green leaf. "How's your potting soil?"

"Good."

"Uh-huh."

Okay. Enough was enough. "What are you trying to tell me?"

Bonnie plopped down on her ancient chaise lounge. "Have a seat."

Gen sat down next to her.

"Let's forget all about those ungrateful plants and focus on you."

"Let's not."

"Too late." Bonnie looked her up and down. "See, the fact of the matter is…I don't think *you're* blooming."

Gen didn't need Bonnie to tell her that. "Are you done?"

"No." Her landlady glanced around the backyard. "Where's Cary?"

"I don't know. I know he's not hiding in the hedge."

"That's not what I meant and you know it. Take pity on an old woman and answer me directly. You two are perfect for each other." She wrinkled her brow. "I thought there was something between you."

"There was. There is."

"So then how come he hasn't been around here lately? How come he's not with you now?"

That's the million-dollar question, isn't it?

Gen had left his classroom with the hope that he'd call, but in the past two days, she'd yet to hear his voice on her phone. "I don't know. Things are confusing."

"Not to my mind."

Bonnie was giving Gen's mother a run for her money. "At my last job—when I was in Cincinnati—there was a cop I was close with." She swallowed, having a hard time even saying his name. "Keaton."

"And?"

"He was a widower. I became his partner after his wife died in a car accident. We became friends. We'd go see movies together, have dinner—all very platonic."

"But—"

"I wanted more. I was sure one day Keaton would stop missing his wife and notice me." Her voice cracked as she recalled her embarrassment. "I waited years. One day, Keaton told me about a woman he'd met. He was smitten. Next thing I knew, he'd stopped grieving for his wife… but had fallen in love with someone else."

"He didn't realize you'd been there the whole time, waiting for him."

"I wasn't the right person for him."

"So you ran away."

She nodded. "I left the CPD and started over here. But, in my defense, I also knew I wanted something different as far as my job. I wanted to work in a smaller town, to feel close to people again."

"But you fought it at first."

"True." Lying back on her chair, holding her face up to the sun, Gen sighed. "I've been constantly wrestling with what I want. One day I'm happy to be single, the next I'm sad. One day I'm making friends, the next I'm putting up roadblocks for anyone who tries to get too close." Straightening, Gen waved a hand. "This is how messed up I've been, Bonnie. When the lieutenant first told me I'd be leaving Lane's End High, I was relieved."

"Because you had a perfect excuse to sever all those friendships in the making."

Gen nodded. "Cary was the most important one. We'd become close, but I started worrying that maybe we'd only become close because we'd been working together, not because there was something really strong and lasting between us."

"What did Cary say?"

"He let me go."

"Well, are you going to try and patch things up?"

"I stopped by his classroom. It's his turn now."

"Don't keep hiding. You're not going to bloom on your own."

Gen grimaced at the metaphor. "What if Cary doesn't think I'm worth it?"

"Let me tell you a secret, Gen. You are completely worth it."

A warm feeling spread through her. As compliments went, most people probably wouldn't have given what Bonnie said a second's thought.

But to Gen it meant the world.

CARY TOOK A LONG sip of Coke, hoping against hope that the current conversation was going to end quickly.

But as Dean argued back and forth with

Melissa, it was obvious that this discussion was set to go on for quite some time.

"Dad, everyone goes to Florida for spring break."

"Not you."

"I'll be perfectly fine. Katie's parents are letting her go."

"All I heard was that Brian was going."

Her cheeks colored. "So?"

"So I don't think the two of you need to be going on vacations together."

"Why?"

When Dean looked his way, Cary grabbed a handful of chips and stuffed a couple in his mouth. Anything to stay out of the exchange.

"You know why," Dean said, his tone firm.

"Because you think Brian and I are going to go too far?"

Ouch. Dean leveled a glance at Melissa. "Yes."

Melissa turned to Cary. "Uncle Cary, say something!"

Cary crammed another chip in his mouth.

"Things can happen on the spur of the moment that you're not ready for," Dean said.

"Oh, Dad. You're treating me like a child. If we wanted to, we'd already be doing it, without you knowing."

Cary just about choked. Man, this was uncomfortable.

"Help me out here, Cary," Dean ordered. "Now."

Dean's standing-on-the-edge-of-a-cliff look made Cary push the chips aside. "Is Brian pressuring you?" Cary said.

"No. He just wants to spend spring break with me."

Dean scowled. "He's lying. I know what's on guys' minds."

"Not yours, Dad. I never see you dating."

Dean paled. "Melissa, you're out of line."

"Well, it's true." She crossed her arms over her chest. "And you're almost as bad, Uncle Cary."

"Hello. I have been dating. Remember Kate? Remember Gen?"

Melissa tossed her head. "Well, you're not dating either of them now."

It was Cary's turn to feel defensive. "That's none of your business."

Dean's expression hardened. "Melissa,

you're staying home on spring break. End of discussion."

Finally Melissa caught on that she'd better not push anymore. "All right."

Dean breathed an audible sigh of relief. Cary lifted his drink in a silent toast.

Until Melissa got started again.

"So what are we doing for Easter?"

"I don't know," Dean said.

"I think we should have a party if I can't go anywhere for spring break."

"Huh?" Dean picked up his pop can, saw that it was empty, then looked to Cary in exasperation.

Cary felt just as confused. "Aren't all your friends going to be in Florida?"

"Actually…there are some other kids who weren't allowed to go, either," Melissa admitted. "And Brian's not exactly sure if his parents will let him."

"*Now* you tell me that."

Melissa shrugged. "So what do you think?" Warming up, she said, "We could buy one of those hams from the deli, and I could make a cake." She turned to Cary. "You can make salad."

Making a salad involved opening two bags. "I can do that."

"Everyone else can bring a dish. We can play badminton or volleyball in the backyard." Eyes shining, she looked to her dad. "Please say yes."

"Yes."

Melissa hopped up with enough speed to make Cary wonder if a party had been in her plans all along. "I'm going to go make the guest list."

As she ran back inside, Cary glanced at his brother. He was clutching his empty pop can and looking as if he'd been through a war. "Ever feel like you've been had?"

"Constantly." Dean shook his head. "My girl is growing up in spite of my best efforts."

"I know."

"Do you think I should have said yes about Florida?"

"No," Cary said, taking another sip. "That sounded like trouble."

After grabbing another pop out of the cooler, Dean took a celebratory sip. "I hate to say it, but Melissa was right. Gen's been pretty nonexistent around here. What's going on?"

"I'm not really sure."

"Why don't you invite her over on Easter?"

"I might do that." Cary looked at his brother. "Maybe you should invite someone, too."

"I would if I had anyone in mind, but I don't."

"That sucks."

Dean nodded. "Melissa has a point. I haven't dated anyone seriously in years. It's gotten ridiculous."

"Not all women are like Valerie."

"Or like Kate."

Cary stood up. "I think I'm going to go make a phone call."

GEN SAT DOWN AS soon as she realized who was on the phone. "Cary, hi."

"Hey, how are you?"

She was exhausted. Though she liked her new job with Mike, the stress of learning the new routine and responsibilities as quickly as possible had been a challenge, but she'd expected that.

What she hadn't expected was feeling so lonely at night. The hours seemed to stretch on forever. Even Sadie moped around the place, obviously missing Sludge.

But she didn't want to admit any of that. "Fine."

"I don't know how to do this any other way—I miss you, Gen."

Tears stung her eyes. "I miss you, too."

"I've been trying to give you more time, like you wanted, but it hasn't been easy."

She didn't want any more time. "I shouldn't have left without trying harder to mend things between us."

"I can't believe we're having this discussion on the phone. I'm coming over, okay?"

"I'll be here," she said, smiling when she realized he'd already hung up.

CARY HAD HAD IT ALL planned. He was going to sit down on Genevieve's ugly couch and hold her hand. Looking into her eyes, he was going to very calmly, very systematically review the reasons they should give their relationship another chance. He was going to tell her he loved her but not push her into admitting anything she wasn't ready for.

And then, only then, was he going to take her in his arms. No way did he want any of this to happen out of order, knowing full well any deviation from the plan would guarantee distraction.

But the moment she opened the door, looking feminine in a little slip of a dress, Cary skipped steps one through four and pulled her into his arms.

She was breathless when their kiss ended. "Wow. Hello."

He tried to look embarrassed. "I'm sorry. I don't know what came over me."

There was that smile again, just touching the corners of her lips but lighting her eyes like a hundred-watt bulb. "Thanks. Um, do you want to sit down?"

She led him to the table, where she'd set out a pot of coffee and some cookies.

"I didn't bake the cookies," Gen pointed out. "Bonnie did. They're really good."

He took one, poured himself a cup of coffee, then sat across from her. "I'm impressed."

"Well..." She shrugged as her voice

trailed off. "I'd like to say something witty in response, but the truth is I'm no good at that. I'm not very good at relationships, period."

"Here's my truth—I don't want to lose you."

"I don't want to lose you, either."

Relief filled him. "So are we good?"

Gen scanned his face, saw everything she'd ever wanted, then nodded. "I can't speak for you, but I'm a yes."

He grinned. "Me, too."

She laughed when he pulled her toward him. Following his lead, she wrapped her arms around him as Cary trailed his fingers down her bare shoulders and along her toned arms. Her body swayed as he held her tightly and kissed her neck.

Cary pulled back slightly. "I almost forgot—Easter."

"Huh?"

"Will you come over to my place for dinner? Melissa's planning the whole thing."

"Sure."

As their lips met again, he caught the

silky fabric of her dress between his fingers. Smiling, he couldn't help teasing her.

"Pink, Gen?"

She shrugged. "Today is my feminine day. Tomorrow it's blue jeans all the way."

CHAPTER TWENTY-TWO

LATER THAT NIGHT, after he'd left Gen's place and gone home, Cary thought about Dean and Melissa again. It was a good thing they'd become more dependent on each other. No matter how crazy this Easter brunch was going to be, Cary had a feeling it represented a turning point for all of them.

Dean asking his new assistant, Dianna Grant, was proof of that. Though Dean hadn't said as much, Cary suspected his brother had strong feelings for the petite brunette. There was something in the way he talked about her that lit him up inside.

It looked as though another chapter was opening for both of them. Time to make some decisions. Time to tell Gen just how much she meant to him.

Time to ask her to marry him and to stay in Lane's End forever. He hoped she'd care enough about him to conquer any old fears.

But, just for added insurance, he called Marilyn Townsend, the dog breeder he'd contacted a few days ago. "Mary, do you still have that pup?"

"I do. She's adorable. I had another call about her last night."

Biting the bullet, he said, "Save her for me, will you?"

Mary's voice became a little tentative. "Are you sure about that, Cary? Sludge is quite a handful."

"I'm sure. I'll be by tomorrow with a check, but I don't want to pick her up her until Easter. Would that be okay?"

"That's fine. I hope Sludge doesn't give her all his bad qualities. It would be a real shame to sell you two pups to ruin."

"Sludge is fine, just mischievous. Besides, the puppy isn't for me, it's for a friend. See you Sunday morning after church?"

After an exaggerated sigh, Mary said, "We'll be ready."

"OH, CARY. SHE'S beautiful!" Gen held Maddie against her chest, wrinkling her nose as the puppy covered Gen's face with excited kisses. "I love her."

"I'm glad." Cary caressed the pup's soft ears as it yipped and squirmed in Gen's arms. Though he'd been pretty sure Gen was going to love the gift, seeing the pure joy on her face when she'd seen the little beribboned dog come scampering her way was something he would never forget.

So far everything was perfect, even the weather. April's arrival had brought with it seventy-degree temperatures and a fresh burst of spring. Sunny-yellow daffodils and pink, white and red tulips were blooming everywhere, making Lane's End—and his backyard—look vibrant and festive.

He and Melissa and Dean had gone a little crazy getting ready for the party. Between mulching beds, trimming bushes and applying a fresh coat of white paint to the back fence, Cary had hardly had a spare minute during the past few days.

As the puppy licked Gen's chin, she looked up at him with the most gorgeous smile he'd ever seen. "You didn't have to do this, you know. Everything's good between us."

"I know. I just wanted a little insurance," he said, kissing Gen's cheek.

"For what?"

"Watch out!" Melissa called as a volleyball sailed toward Gen, cutting off any forthcoming reply.

Cary pulled Gen and the puppy to him just before the white ball flew by. "Watch it!"

"Sorry!" Brian called out.

"You okay?" Cary asked, relaxing his grip on her but keeping her close.

"Sure," she said with a smile. "Both Maddie and I are."

He brushed his lips against her brow. "So…Maddie?"

"Yep. For 'Madness.' Getting another dog is madness…but I can't resist her."

Maddie barked. After Gen set her down, the tiny beagle padded toward Dianna, Dean's assistant.

Watching Dianna pick up the pup while she chatted with Bonnie and Christy, Gen smiled. "I think Dianna's having a good time. I'm so glad she came."

"I am, too. It's nice to see Dean with a

date, even though he's saying there's nothing between them."

Gen nodded. "Don't be so sure. There's something there, and my guess is that it's more than just work-related. I've spied each of them sneaking peeks at the other when they thought no one was looking."

He couldn't resist teasing her. "Always a cop?"

Her eyes glowed. "Almost always a cop. Sometimes, though, I'm just Gen."

There was nothing "just" about her. In fact, when Cary looked at her, he felt that she was everything.

Glancing around, Cary knew this was the perfect time to propose. Everyone he and Gen cared about was nearby...and everyone was also busy enough to not be paying attention to every movement they made.

"Let's sit over here." He gestured toward an empty wrought-iron bench nestled next to a trio of bright blue ceramic pots. After they sat, he took her hands in his. "Before I met you, I didn't know how much was missing in my life. I thought everything was perfect—well, as good as it was going to get."

Her eyes widened as he continued. "You've made me think about a lot of things—about what makes me happy, what makes me want to get up in the morning. It's like that crazy basketball tournament, Gen. Who would have ever thought we'd go all the way to state? Who would have ever thought the whole town would come together the way it did? It was exciting and scary and nerve-racking, but I'd never change the experience for anything. I want those feelings with you, Gen. I want to have it all."

The smile she treated him to was worth all the idiotic confessions in the world.

"I love you, Gen."

"I love you, too."

"I want to marry you."

"Me, too," she said glibly, then clasped a hand over her mouth. "Oh! I can't believe I just said that…like that!"

With a laugh, she said, "Yes, I will marry you." She leaned forward to press her lips against his cheek, his jaw, his mouth.

Cary wrapped her up in his arms—just

as he realized that the rest of the partygoers had stopped everything they were doing and were crowding around them. Clapping.

"It's about time," Bonnie said.

"I knew we needed champagne!" Christy called out. "Dave, come help me."

"I can't believe you proposed to her *here,*" Dean said. "Don't you think a little privacy would have been nice?"

Cary turned to Gen. "Did I do this all wrong?"

"Are you kidding? We're together, our friends are here…you gave me a puppy! Your proposal was perfect."

Christy hugged her. "Congratulations. You two will be perfect together."

When Melissa strode forward, worry etched on her features, Gen started to regret that they'd done things so publicly. But then Melissa launched herself into Cary's arms, hugging him as if she were six years old again.

"I'm so happy!" Melissa exclaimed.

Cary held her close. "Me, too. Today couldn't get any better."

Two shrill barks pierced the air.

Dean's expression turned to pure panic. "Sadie! Sludge! No!"

As if in slow motion, the whole group turned to the wide, grassy area where the beagles were playing—with a very large, very expensive honey-baked ham.

Actually, calling it "playing" was rather generous. Sadie and Sludge were clawing and tearing at that poor piece of ham as if they were wolves and they didn't want to share the ham with the rest of the pack.

Not to be outdone, Maddie, their new apprentice, was eating a puppy-size chunk and growling with all her might.

"That breeder is going to kill me," Cary said with a groan.

A MULTITUDE OF things happened at once. Cary ran over to the dogs and attempted to remove them from the ham.

Melissa burst into tears.

And people started noticing that things were missing. The eggs were gone—a lot of eggs were gone.

So was a big hunk of Bonnie's baked ziti.

Shredded ribbon marked the place where

stuffed Easter bunnies had once stood proudly.

And all that was left of the lamb-shaped Jell-O mold was its head, cherry-red gelatin oozing as if it had been decapitated.

Dean muttered something about beagles, and everyone was spurred into action. Bonnie herded Sadie and Sludge. Christy scooped up Maddie. Brian tried to control his laughing while trying to comfort a still-upset Melissa.

And Cary looked as if he might abandon them all.

Clearly, it was up to Gen to restore order. Slipping her first and fourth fingers into her mouth, she expertly let out a sharp whistle. The result was shrill and loud enough to stop everyone in their tracks.

Even Sadie and Sludge forgot about the ham for a moment.

"Cary, grab those dogs and kennel them."

Once she saw that both beagles' collars were firmly in Cary's large hands, she turned to everyone else. "Let's get this mess cleaned up. Melissa, go get two large garbage bags."

"But, Officer Slate—"

"It's Gen," she corrected with a small smile. "Let's tidy up, then reconvene in the kitchen."

Finally Gen turned to everyone else who was either looking around in shock or valiantly trying not to laugh at the state of the party.

After a brief pause, Christy motioned to the metal tub filled with soda and four bottles of champagne. "As far as I'm concerned, if there's still something to toast with, there's still a reason to have a party."

Someone turned on the music, and everyone's voices rose accordingly.

Gen heaved a sigh of relief as she saw Cary loping toward her. "How are the dogs?"

He rolled his eyes. "About what you'd expect. They're irritated to be back in the kennel but too full to do much except groan and lie on their sides."

"Poor things."

"Don't feel sorry for them for a second. Serves them right." He shook his head in dismay. "I'd say I couldn't believe what they just did, but I'd be lying. These are the type of shenanigans Sludge excels at."

"Sadie's no different. And, unfortunately, I think they found a worthy trainee in Maddie."

Cary wrapped an arm around her. "Where were we?"

She smiled. "Getting engaged. I believe you were kissing me."

He leaned closer. "I think I remember that."

Gazing up at him, she said, "I love you."

"I love you, too," he whispered, pressing his lips to hers.

Oh! She pulled away. "I almost forgot to tell you—my Easter lilies bloomed today."

Gently enfolding her in his arms, Cary said, "Well, that just about makes our day complete."

As their lips met again, Gen felt the warmth of the sun and the promise of a bright future. April was here and May was right around the corner.

It looked as though March and all its

madness was over, and her life—the life she'd always dreamed of having—was just about to begin.

* * * * *

REQUEST YOUR FREE BOOKS!
2 FREE WHOLESOME ROMANCE NOVELS
IN LARGER PRINT
PLUS 2
FREE
MYSTERY GIFTS

⚜️⚜️⚜️⚜️⚜️⚜️⚜️⚜️⚜️⚜️⚜️⚜️⚜️⚜️⚜️⚜️

HEARTWARMING™

Wholesome, tender romances

HWDIR13

LARGER-PRINT BOOKS!

GET 2 FREE LARGER-PRINT NOVELS PLUS 2 FREE MYSTERY GIFTS

Love Inspired®

Larger-print novels are now available...

YES! Please send me 2 FREE LARGER-PRINT Love Inspired® novels and my 2 FREE mystery gifts (gifts are worth about $10). After receiving them, if I don't wish to receive any more books, I can return the shipping statement marked "cancel." If I don't cancel, I will receive 6 brand-new novels every month and be billed just $4.99 per book in the U.S. or $5.49 per book in Canada. That's a savings of at least 23% off the cover price. It's quite a bargain! Shipping and handling is just 50¢ per book in the U.S. and 75¢ per book in Canada.* I understand that accepting the 2 free books and gifts places me under no obligation to buy anything. I can always return a shipment and cancel at any time. Even if I never buy another book, the two free books and gifts are mine to keep forever.

122/322 IDN FVY7

Name	(PLEASE PRINT)	
Address		Apt. #
City	State/Prov.	Zip/Postal Code

Signature (if under 18, a parent or guardian must sign)

Mail to the **Harlequin® Reader Service:**
IN U.S.A.: P.O. Box 1867, Buffalo, NY 14240-1867
IN CANADA: P.O. Box 609, Fort Erie, Ontario L2A 5X3

Are you a current subscriber to Love Inspired books and want to receive the larger-print edition?
Call 1-800-873-8635 or visit www.ReaderService.com.

* Terms and prices subject to change without notice. Prices do not include applicable taxes. Sales tax applicable in N.Y. Canadian residents will be charged applicable taxes. Offer not valid in Quebec. This offer is limited to one order per household. Not valid for current subscribers to Love Inspired Larger Print books. All orders subject to credit approval. Credit or debit balances in a customer's account(s) may be offset by any other outstanding balance owed by or to the customer. Please allow 4 to 6 weeks for delivery. Offer available while quantities last.

Your Privacy—The Harlequin® Reader Service is committed to protecting your privacy. Our Privacy Policy is available online at www.ReaderService.com or upon request from the Harlequin Reader Service.

We make a portion of our mailing list available to reputable third parties that offer products we believe may interest you. If you prefer that we not exchange your name with third parties, or if you wish to clarify or modify your communication preferences, please visit us at www.ReaderService.com/consumerchoice or write to us at Harlequin Reader Service Preference Service, P.O. Box 9062, Buffalo, NY 14269. Include your complete name and address.

LILPDIR13